MP3

別再笑, 「他媽的」 英文怎麼說?

U0088383

將徹底改變
你的錯誤觀念與用法
一次全收錄你想像不到的口語用法!

英文會有多難?只要掌握**必學的口語英文**,
人人都可以輕鬆開口說英文!

Note

英文學習一把罩,最道地的口語化英文!

有一些很簡單的英文,平時可能使用的機會不多,但是等到真正要表達時,卻怎麼想都想不起來!

或是某些口語化英文好像曾經聽過、又很熟悉,例如:「他媽的」、「少管閒事」、「禁足」、「我挺你」等,但是老師根本沒有教過啊!這時候該怎麼辦呢?

針對上述的種種疑惑,本書「別再笑,『他媽的』英文怎麼說?」提出了全方位的解決方案!本書收納了超過2百句的口語化實用英文,一次全收錄你想像不到的實用、道地的口語用法!是學校課堂上學不到的精華內容,搭配實用會話例句,讓您徹底瞭解運用的時機,也才能夠學會正統的生活英文用語。

此外，本書還隨書附贈學習MP3 光碟，讓您英文學習一把罩！隨著外籍導讀師的語氣、腔調、速度練習口語化英文，建議您邊聽邊開口大聲隨讀，學習效果一定能事半功倍，以加強您的口語英文實力。

英文會有多難？只要掌握必學的口語英文，人人都可以輕鬆開口説英文！

Note

2

他媽的！
Damn it.

會話實例

A Damn it.
他媽的！

B What's wrong? It's about Jack again?
怎麼啦？又是和傑克有關嗎？

A No. It's about my salary.
不是，是和我的薪水有關！

會話實例

A God damn it.
該死！

B Come on, it's not your fault.
不要這樣，不是你的錯啊！

A I know.
我知道啊！

你去死吧！
Go to hell.

會話實例

A Go away.
你走開！

B What the...
你真是…

A Go to hell.
你去死吧！

會話實例

A Don't be so sad!
不要這麼難過啦！

B Go to hell.
你去死吧！

A What did you just say?
你剛剛說什麼？

🎧 3

糟糕！
Shit.

會話實例

A Shit.
　糟糕！

B I beg your pardon?
　你說什麼？

會話實例

A Shit. It's all over now.
　糟糕！全毀了！

B Come on. You're still young.
　不要這樣嘛！你還年輕啊！

會話實例

A Check this out.
　你看！

B Shit. What happened?
　糟糕！發生什麼事了？

變態！
Sick.

A Maybe you wanna stay here with me.

也許你想留下來陪我！

B Sick.

你變態啊！

A Did you see that old guy?

你有看見那個老傢伙嗎？

B Oh, sick.

喔，真變態！

A Look at this, buddy.

兄弟，看這個！

B Wow, I'm going to get sick.

哇，好噁心！

🔊 4

唉呀！
My, my.

會話實例

A My, my. It's good to see you again.
唉呀！真高興又見到你！

B Me too.
我也很高興！

會話實例

A My, my. You're a big boy now, aren't you?
唉呀！你變成了個大男孩了，對嗎？

B Who are you?
你是誰？

A It's me! Your Uncle Jack.
是我啊！傑克叔叔啊！

糟透了！
Sucks.

會話實例

A What do you think of the movie?
你覺得這部電影好看嗎？

B Sucks.
糟透了！

會話實例

A What do you think of my idea?
你覺得我的想法怎麼樣？

B It sucks.
糟透了！

會話實例

A Well, how would you like it?
呃，你喜歡嗎？

B No, it sucks.
不喜歡，它糟透了！

🌀 5

拜託啦！
Please?

會話實例

A Can I play baseball?
我可以玩棒球嗎？

B No way.
不可以！

A Please?
拜託啦！

會話實例

A I need to see Jack.
我得要去和傑克見面。

B We'll see.
再說吧！

A Please?
拜託啦！

別跟我胡扯！
Don't give me your shit.

A I'll kick your ass.
我會揍扁你！

B Don't give me your shit.
別跟我胡扯！

A I think it's a good idea.
我覺得是個好主意！

B Don't give me your shit.
別跟我胡扯！

A Don't give me your shit.
別跟我胡扯！

B Excuse me?
你說什麼？

🔊 6

那是什麼鬼東西？
What the hell was that?

會話實例

A What the hell was that?
那是什麼鬼東西？

B What? What did you see?
什麼？你看見什麼了？

會話實例

A What the hell was that?
那是什麼鬼東西？

B A tiger?
是一隻老虎嗎？

會話實例

A Check this out.
你看！

B What the hell was that?
那是什麼鬼東西？

真是難為你了！
It's not easy for you.

會話實例

A I can't take it anymore.
我再也受不了了！

B I know. It's not easy for you.
我知道。真是難為你了！

會話實例

A It's not easy for you.
真是難為你了！

B Not at all. Anyway, thank you for everything.
一點都不會啦！總之，凡事多謝了！

會話實例

A It's not easy for you.
真是難為你了！

B It's nothing.
沒什麼啊！

🔊 7

這才像話！
Now you're talking.

會話實例

A Would you like pizza for dinner?
你晚餐要吃披薩嗎？

B Now you're talking.
這樣說才像話嘛！

會話實例

A Here you are. These are my new co-mic books.
給你！這些是我新的漫畫。

B Now you're talking!
這才像話呀！

會話實例

A Why don't we accept his idea?
我們何不接受他的主意？

B Now you're talking!
這才像話呀！

祝你今天順利！
Have a good day.

A Have a good day.
祝你今天順利！

B Thanks a lot! Bye.
多謝啦！再見！

A Have a good day.
祝你今天順利！

B You too.
你也是(要順利)啊！

A Got to go now.
我得走啦！

B Sure. Have a good day.
好啊！祝你今天順利！

8

我沒有這個打算。
I wasn't planning on it.

會話實例

A Do you wanna go with us?
你想和我們去嗎？

B NO. I wasn't planning on it.
沒有！我沒有這個打算。

會話實例

A Maybe it's good for you, right?
也許對你來說是好事，對嗎？

B Who knows? I wasn't planning on it.
誰知道？我沒有這個打算。

會話實例

A I wasn't planning on it.
我沒有這個打算。

B Why not? You just let her go?
為什麼不要？你就這樣讓她離開？

有道理！
Fair enough.

會話實例

A Let's divide up the work.
我們平均分配工作吧！

B Fair enough.
有道理！

會話實例

A We've decided to send it back.
我們已經決定要把它送回去。

B Fair enough.
有道理！

會話實例

A We gave up.
我們放棄了！

B Fair enough.
很公平啊！

9

你變了！
You've changed.

會話實例

A I just can't leave it alone.
我就是無法置之不理。

B You've changed.
你變了！

會話實例

A You've changed.
你變了！

B Me? What makes you think so?
我？你為什麼會這麼認為？

會話實例

A You've changed.
你變了！

B I am not.
我沒有！

我不想打官司。
I don't wanna go to court.

會話實例

A What would you do with it?
你會怎麼處理？

B I don't wanna go to court.
我不想打官司。

會話實例

A I don't wanna go to court.
我不想打官司。

B You have no choice.
你別無選擇！

會話實例

A I just don't wanna go to court.
我就是不想打官司。

B You don't have to unless you give it back to us.
你可以不用，除非你把它還給我們！

🔵 10

你只能靠你自己了！
You're on your own.

會話實例

A What am I supposed to do?
我該怎麼辦？

B You're on your own.
你只能靠你自己了！

會話實例

A Please! Don't leave me.
拜託！不要離開我！

B You're on your own now.
你現在只能靠你自己了！

會話實例

A You're on your own.
你只能靠你自己了！

B Come on, pal, it's not my fault.
拜託，兄弟，這不是我的錯啊！

你睡著了！
You fell asleep.

會話實例

A Hey!
嘿！

B What? What's wrong?
什麼？怎麼了？

A You fell asleep.
你睡著了！

會話實例

A Wake up. You fell asleep.
醒一醒！你睡著了！

B Oh, sorry.
喔，抱歉！

會話實例

A You fell asleep.
你睡著了！

B Really? What time is it?
真的嗎？幾點了？

11

一點都不像你！
Kind of unlike you.

會話實例

A I won't go with them.
我不會和他們去！

B Kind of unlike you.
一點都不像你！

A What do you mean?
你是什麼意思？

會話實例

A I changed my mind.
我改變主意了！

B Kind of unlike you.
一點都不像你！

A Why not?
為什麼不像我？

我剛剛滑倒了！
I just slipped.

會話實例

A Are you OK?
你還好嗎？

B I just slipped.
我剛剛滑倒了！

會話實例

A What happened to you?
你怎麼啦？

B I just slipped.
我剛剛滑倒了！

會話實例

A I just slipped.
我剛剛滑倒了！

B I told you to be careful.
我告訴過你要小心一點！

🔵 12

你要對我說謊嗎？
You're gonna lie to me?

會話實例

A Are you OK?
你還好嗎？

B I'm fine.
我沒事！

A You're gonna lie to me?
你要對我說謊嗎？

會話實例

A It's no big deal.
沒什麼大不了啊！

B You're gonna lie to me?
你要對我說謊嗎？

A No, I am not.
沒有，我哪有！

我正在想辦法解決！
I'm trying to work things out.

會話實例

A What now?
現在該怎麼辦？

B I'm trying to work things out.
我正在想辦法解決！

會話實例

A I'm trying to work things out.
我正在想辦法解決！

B And then?
然後呢？

會話實例

A I'm trying to work things out.
我正在想辦法解決！

B Good. What are you gonna do?
很好！你打算怎麼做？

13

你去哪裡了？
Where have you been?

會話實例

A I'm home.
我回來囉！

B Where have you been?
你去哪裡了？

會話實例

A Where have you been?
你去哪裡了？

B I went for a run.
我去散步了！

會話實例

A Where have you been?
你去哪裡了？

B I've been to New York to visit my parents.
我去了趟紐約探望我的父母。

我們需要聊一聊！
We need to talk.

會話實例

A Are you OK?
你還好吧？

B We need to talk.
我們需要聊一聊！

會話實例

A Something wrong?
有問題嗎？

B Yeah. Got a minute? We need to talk.
是啊！你有空嗎？我們需要聊一聊！

會話實例

A We need to talk.
我們需要聊一聊！

B Sure. Come on in.
好啊！進來吧！

● 14

都告訴我吧！
Tell me all about it.

會話實例

A What do you want to know?
你想知道些什麼？

B Tell me all about it.
都告訴我吧！

會話實例

A Tell me all about it.
都告訴我吧！

B No, I don't think so.
不要，我不想要！

會話實例

A Tell me all about it.
都告訴我吧！

B Sure. You got it.
好啊！就依你！

很遺憾你這麼認為！
I'm sorry you feel that way.

會話實例

A I think it's her. Right?
我覺得就是她，對嗎？

B I'm sorry you feel that way.
很遺憾你這麼認為！

會話實例

A I thought it's nothing at all.
我以為都沒事！

B I'm sorry you feel that way.
很遺憾你這麼認為！

會話實例

A I'm sorry you feel that way.
很遺憾你這麼認為！

B It doesn't matter.
沒關係！

● 15

你不可以放棄！
Don't you give up?

會話實例

A Never mind. I don't wanna talk about it now.
不用在意！我現在不想談！

B Don't you give up?
你不可以放棄！

會話實例

A Don't you give up?
你不可以放棄。

B Why not?
為什麼不可以？

會話實例

A Don't you give up?
你不可以放棄！

B I know, but I don't know what to do.
我知道，但是我不知道該怎麼辦！

你懂嗎？
Do you understand?

會話實例

A Do you understand?
你懂嗎？

B Yes, sir.
是的，長官。

會話實例

A Do you understand?
你懂嗎？

B Yes, I understand.
知道，我瞭解！

會話實例

A Do you understand?
你懂嗎？

B No, I'm still confused.
不懂，我還是很困惑！

🔊 16

讓我說句話!
Let me say something.

會話實例

A What? What do you want?
什麼?你想要什麼?

B Let me say something.
讓我說句話!

會話實例

A Let me say something.
讓我說句話!

B No way.
免談!

會話實例

A Let me just say something.
讓我說句話!

B Shoot.
說吧!

你瘋啦？
Are you completely mad?

會話實例

A I'm not one of your people.
我不是你們的人。

B Are you completely mad?
你瘋啦？

會話實例

A Are you completely mad?
你瘋啦？

B No, I am not. You are.
沒有，我沒有！是你瘋了！

會話實例

A Are you mad?
你瘋啦？

B So what? I'm not coming.
那又怎麼樣？我不會去！

17

你是瘋了還是怎麼了？
Are you crazy or what?

會話實例

A Hey, pal, just let her in.
嘿，兄弟，讓她進來！

B Are you crazy or what?
你是瘋了還是怎麼了？

會話實例

A This is what we're gonna do.
我們就是要這麼做！

B Are you crazy or what?
你是瘋了還是怎麼了？

會話實例

A What? Are you crazy or what?
什麼嘛！你是瘋了還是怎麼了？

B Don't worry about me.
不用擔心我啦！

歷史會重演。
History repeats itself.

會話實例

A History repeats itself.
歷史會重演。

B Come on, it's not so serious.
別這樣！沒這麼嚴重！

會話實例

A What happened, happened.
事情已經發生了！

B But don't you think history repeats itself?
我知道，但你不認為歷史會重演嗎？

會話實例

A History repeats itself.
歷史會重演。

B I don't understand. About what?
我不懂！關於什麼事？

18

我覺得我辦得到！
I think I can do that.

會話實例

A Well... say something.
嗯，說句話啊！

B I think I can do that.
我覺得我辦得到！

會話實例

A I think I can do that.
我覺得我辦得到！

B What would you do?
你會怎麼做？

會話實例

A I think I can do that.
我覺得我辦得到！

B Are you sure about it?
你有確定嗎？

你相信我嗎？
Do you trust me?

A Do you trust me?
你相信我嗎？

B No, I don't.
不，我不相信！

A Come on, you have no choice.
拜託！你別無選擇！

A What now?
現在怎麼辦？

B Do you trust me?
你相信我嗎？

A Yes, I do.
是啊，我相信你！

19

沒有幫助的。
It doesn't help.

會話實例

A Maybe we can fix it.
也許我們可以修好！

B It doesn't help.
沒有幫助的。

會話實例

A Let me take a look at it.
給我看一下！

B It doesn't help.
沒有幫助的。

會話實例

A It doesn't help.
沒有幫助的。

B How would you know?
你怎麼會知道？

我一定會出席。
I'll be there.

會話實例

A Will you come over?
你會來嗎？

B I'll be there.
我一定會出席。

會話實例

A I'll be there.
我一定會出席。

B OK. See you then.
好，到時候再見！

會話實例

A I'll be there.
我一定會出席。

B Sure, I'll meet you there.
好，到時候在那裡見囉！

🔊 20

哪有這麼好的事！
It's too good to be true.

會話實例

A Look what I got from Jack.
你看我從傑克那裡拿了這個。

B Wow, it's too good to be true.
哇！哪有這麼好的事！

會話實例

A We won the game.
我們贏了這場比賽！

B It's too good to be true.
哪有這麼好的事！

會話實例

A Don't you think it's too good to be true?
你不認為哪有這麼好的事嗎？

B So what?
那又怎麼樣？

我只是隨口問問。
Just checking.

A What makes you think so?
你為什麼會這麼想？

B Just checking.
我只是隨口問問。

A OK. You got it.
好，就讓你知道！

A Just checking.
我只是隨口問問。

B Yes?
要問什麼事？

A Are you seeing someone?
你有交往的對象嗎？

21

好巧啊！
What a coincidence.

會話實例

A Jack? Is that you?
傑克？是你嗎？

B Hi, Maggie, I never thought that I'd see you here.
嗨，瑪姬，沒想到會在這裡遇見妳。

會話實例

A What a coincidence.
好巧啊！

B Jack! I haven't seen you for ages.
傑克！真是好久不見了。

會話實例

A Whoa! What a coincidence.
哇！好巧啊！

B Yeah! What happened, happened.
是啊，事情已經發生了！

久仰大名！
I've heard a lot about you.

會話實例

A I've heard a lot about you.
久仰大名！

B Really? Was it good or bad?
真的啊？都聽說了什麼好事還是壞事？

會話實例

A I've heard a lot about you.
久仰大名！

B Nothing bad, I hope.
希望沒有什麼壞事！

A He told me so much about you.
他告訴我好多有關你的事。

22

我對這裡也不熟。
I'm a stranger here myself.

會話實例

A Excuse me, would you give me some directions?

請問一下，你可以指引我方向嗎？

B Sorry. I'm a stranger here myself.

抱歉！我對這裡也不熟。

會話實例

A Could you tell me where the bank is?

請問銀行在哪裡？

B Sorry. I'm a stranger here myself.

抱歉！我對這裡也不熟。

會話實例

A Do you know where we are now?

你知道我們現在人在哪裡嗎？

B I'm a stranger here myself.

我對這裡也不熟。

什麼時間合適呢？
What time will it be all right?

會話實例

A What time will it be all right?
什麼時間合適呢？

B I'd say ten thirty.
我認為十點半。

A OK. You got it.
好，就這麼辦！

會話實例

A What time will it be all right?
什麼時間合適呢？

B How about 8 pm?
晚上八點鐘好嗎？

A Great! See you around.
好！回頭見！

🔊 23

我不敢相信我所看到的！
I can't believe my eyes!

會話實例

A Check this out!
你看！

B Whoa! I can't believe my eyes!
哇！我不敢相信我所看到的！

會話實例

A I can't believe my eyes!
我不敢相信我所看到的！

B What? What happened?
什麼？發生什麼事了？

會話實例

A I can't believe my eyes!
我不敢相信我所看到的！

B Neither can I.
我也是！

你是知道的。
You know that.

會話實例

A You know that.
你是知道的。

B No, I don't.
不,我不知道!

會話實例

A How come?
為什麼呢?

B I have been busy. You know that.
我一直很忙。你是知道的。

會話實例

A Did he ask you for a ride into town?
他有要求搭你的便車進城嗎?

B Well... you know that.
這個嘛…你是知道的。

A No, I don't really know.
沒有,我完全不知道!

24

希望你是對的！
I hope you are right.

會話實例

A Maybe they just went to the beach.
也許他們去海灘了！

B I hope you are right.
希望你是對的！

會話實例

A I'm sure about that.
我對那件事很確定！

B I hope you are right.
希望你是對的！

會話實例

A I hope you are right.
希望你是對的！

B Of course I am.
當然我是對的！

我猜也是如此。
I guess so.

會話實例

A They're gone. Really!
他們離開了！真的！

B I guess so.
我猜也是如此。

會話實例

A I'm sure that they decided not to move on.
我確定他們決定不要繼續往前走了！

B I guess so.
我猜也是如此。

會話實例

A I guess so. Right?
我猜也是如此。對吧？

B No, it can't be.
不，不可能！

25

> # 我想是如此吧！
> ## I think so.

會話實例

A Don't go inside. It's a trap.
不要進去！那是個陷阱！

B Yeah, I think so.
是啊，我想是如此吧！

會話實例

A I think so.
我想是如此吧！

B But I think not.
但是我不這麼認為！

會話實例

A It's a good idea.
這是個好主意！

B I think so too.
我想也是如此。

你說的一點都沒錯！
You bet.

會話實例

A Is this is the way to the beach?
這是往海灘的路嗎？

B You bet.
沒錯！

會話實例

A Are you gonna fire me?
你要炒我魷魚嗎？

B You bet.
沒錯！

會話實例

A This is your decision?
這就是你的決定？

B Yeah, you bet.
是啊，沒錯！

26

八字還沒一撇呢！
It's still up in the air.

會話實例

A Are you dating Maggie now?
你和瑪姬在交往嗎？

B It's still up in the air.
八字還沒一撇呢！

會話實例

A Did you decide to settle down?
你有決定要定下來嗎？

B Probably. It's still up in the air.
大概吧。八字還沒一撇呢！

會話實例

A What did they say?
他們說了什麼？

B No idea. It's still up in the air.
不知道！八字還沒一撇呢！

我也是。
Same here.

A I have to go to bed now.
我該去睡覺了。

B Same here.
我也是。

A I'll take this one.
我選這一個！

B Same here.
我也是。

A How about this one? What do you think?
這個好嗎？你覺得呢？

B Same here.
我也是。

27

這行不通的！
It won't work.

會話實例

A Just give it back to me.
還給我！

B It won't work, you know.
你是知道的，這行不通的！

會話實例

A It won't work.
這行不通的！

B Then why would she do that?
那麼她為什麼會那麼做？

會話實例

A It won't work.
這行不通的！

B So what? It's so unfair.
那又怎麼樣？很不公平！

我凡事都會事先計畫好！
I always have a plan.

會話實例

A What shall we do now?
我們現在該怎麼辦？

B Don't worry. I always have a plan.
別擔心！我凡事都會事先計畫好！

會話實例

A I always have a plan.
我凡事都會事先計畫好！

B What plan? You don't even know where we are now.
什麼計畫？你甚至不知道我們現在身在何處。

會話實例

A I always have a plan.
我凡事都會事先計畫好！

B Good. Then what?
很好！那該怎麼辦？

🔴 28

有一會兒了！
A while.

會話實例

A When did you come back?
你什麼時候回來的？

B A while.
有一會兒了！

會話實例

A How long have you been there?
你在那裡待多久了？

B A while.
有一會兒了！

會話實例

A How long are you gonna stay with your parents?
你要和你的父母住多久？

B A while, I guess.
我猜要一陣子吧！

除了這個，其它都行。
Everything but this.

會話實例

A What do you think?
你覺得如何？

B Everything but this.
除了這個，其它都行。

會話實例

A How would you like it?
你喜歡嗎？

B Well, I don't know. Everything but this.
嗯，我不知道耶！除了這個，其它都行。

會話實例

A Are you going to the museum?
你有要去博物館嗎？

B No. Everywhere but this.
沒有，除了這個地方，其它都行。

🌑 29

我錯過了什麼嗎？
Did I miss something?

會話實例

A It's you!
就是你！

B No, not me. Really!
不，不是我！真的！

C Did I miss something?
我錯過了什麼嗎？

會話實例

A Shit!
糟糕！

B Did I miss something?
這是怎麼回事？

A Oh, nothing serious.
喔，沒什麼嚴重的事啦！

我們有達成共識嗎？
Do we have a deal?

A Do we have a deal?
我們有達成共識嗎？

B Yeah, why not.
是啊，沒錯啊！

A Deal?
我們有達成共識嗎？

B Of course.
當然啊！

A Then we have a deal?
那麼我們有達成共識嗎？

B No! No! No! It's not what I meant.
沒有！我不是這個意思！

30

你太過分了。
You're away too far.

會話實例

A This is what I am gonna do.
我就是要這麼做！

B You're away too far.
你太過分了。

會話實例

A You're away too far.
你太過分了。

B So what? You can call the cop.
那又怎麼樣？你可以報警啊！

會話實例

A You're away too far.
你太過分了。

B It's none of your business.
不關你的事！

不錯。
Not bad.

會話實例

A Check this out.
你看！

B Whoa! Not bad.
哇！不錯喔！

會話實例

A What do you think of it?
你覺得如何？

B Not bad, I guess.
我覺得不錯喔！

會話實例

A Not bad, man.
兄弟，不錯喔！

B You think so?
你這麼認為嗎？

🔘 31

我的錯！
My mistake.

會話實例

A My mistake.
我的錯！

B Don't worry about it.
不用擔心啦！

會話實例

A Sorry.
抱歉！

B No. it's my mistake.
不，是我的錯！

會話實例

A Sorry, my mistake.
抱歉，我的錯！

B Hey, man, it's nothing. Really.
嘿，兄弟，沒事啦！真的！

我可以自己處理！
I am OK.

會話實例

A Is it all right?
沒關係嗎？

B I am OK.
我可以自己處理！

會話實例

A Do you need any help?
你需要幫忙嗎？

B I am OK.
我可以自己處理！

會話實例

A Let me help you with it.
我來幫你。

B Thanks. I am OK.
謝謝！我可以自己處理！

🔵 32

你趕著要去哪裡？
What's the rush?

會話實例

A Got to go now.
我現在得走了！

B What's the rush?
你趕著要去哪裡？

會話實例

A What's the rush?
你趕著要去哪裡？

B I have to run an errand.
我要去辦一點事！

會話實例

A What's the rush?
你趕著要去哪裡？

B I'm late for the sales meeting.
我參加銷售會議要遲到了！

好久不見！
Long time no see.

會話實例

A You must be Jack.
你一定是傑克。

B Maggie! Long time no see.
瑪姬！好久不見！

會話實例

A Long time no see.
好久不見！

B Yeah, since you left Taipei.
是啊，自從你離開台北後！

會話實例

A Long time no see.
好久不見！

B Yeah. What a coincidence.
是啊！好巧啊！

🔵 33

誰知道？
Who knows?

會話實例

A Where is Jack?
傑克人在哪裡？

B Who knows?
誰知道？

會話實例

A What are they gonna do with it?
他們要怎麼處理？

B Who knows?
誰知道？

會話實例

A You don't know?
你不知道？

B Who knows?
誰知道？

你少管閒事！
It's none of your busi-ness.

會話實例

A It's none of your business.
你少管閒事！

B Don't ever say that again.
不要再這麼說了！

會話實例

A It's none of your business.
你少管閒事！

B Fine.
隨便你！

會話實例

A You should eat something.
你應該吃點東西。

B None of your business.
不關你的事！

🔊 34

真是無藥可救！
Helpless.

會話實例

A I am fine. Don't worry about me.
我很好！不用擔心我啦！

B Helpless.
你真是無藥可救！

會話實例

A Helpless.
真是無藥可救！

B So what?
那又怎麼樣？

會話實例

A Helpless.
真是無藥可救！

B Leave me alone.
你不要管我！

我沒那個美國時間！
I don't have so much time.

會話實例

A Why don't you do your homework?
你為什麼不寫作業？

B I don't have so much time.
我沒那個美國時間！

會話實例

A Maybe you can call him for help.
也許你可以打電話給他請求幫忙！

B I don't have so much time.
我沒那個美國時間！

會話實例

A Don't you think it's too late?
你不覺得太晚了嗎？

B So what? I don't have so much time.
那又怎麼樣？我沒那個美國時間！

🔵 35

我餓斃了！
I'm so starving.

會話實例

A Is there any food to eat? I'm so starving.

有吃的嗎？我餓斃了！

B Let me make you a sandwich.

我幫你做一個三明治。

會話實例

A I'm so starving.

我餓斃了！

B Let's get something to eat.

我們找點東西來吃。

會話實例

A What would you like to have?

你想吃點什麼？

B Anything. I'm so starving.

什麼都好！我餓斃了！

不要再囉唆了！
Say no more.

會話實例

A You're not listening to me.
你都沒在聽我説！

B Say no more.
不要再囉唆了！

會話實例

A Say no more.
不要再囉唆了！

B Hey, I am your mother.
嘿，我是你媽耶！

會話實例

A It's late now. It may take thirty minutes or more.
現在很晚了！可能需要卅分鐘或更久的時間。

B Say no more.
不要再囉唆了！

● 36

給你！
Here you are.

會話實例

A May I see your passport?
請給我看你的護照！

B Sure. Here you are.
好的！給你！

會話實例

A Here you are. Keep the change.
給你！不用找零錢了！

B Thank you.
謝謝你。

會話實例

A Here you are.
我幫你！

B Thanks! It's not easy to open it.
謝謝！要打開真不容易！

你說呢？
You tell me.

會話實例

A Wrong?
不對嗎？

B You tell me.
你說呢？

會話實例

A Shit! What the hell was that?
可惡！那是什麼鬼東西？

B You tell me.
你說呢？

會話實例

A How about you?
你的看法呢？

B You tell me.
你說呢？

🔵 37

隨便你！
It's up to you.

會話實例

A I don't wanna go with you.
我不想和你一起去！

B Fine. It's up to you.
很好！隨便你！

會話實例

A Up to you.
隨便你！

B Come on, buddy, say something.
老兄，不要這樣嘛，說說你的意見嘛！

會話實例

A I gotta get out of here.
我得趕緊閃人了！

B Up to you.
隨便你！

小事一樁！
It's a piece of cake.

會話實例

A Can you do it for me?
可以幫我做嗎？

B It's a piece of cake.
小事一樁！

會話實例

A Please?
拜託囉？

B Sure. It's a piece of cake.
好啊！小事一樁！

A Thank you so much.
非常感謝你！

會話實例

A Do you mind?
你介意嗎？

B No, not at all. A piece of cake.
不會啦！小事一樁！

38

你腦袋有問題啊？
What's your problem?

會話實例

A It's about Maggie, Jack's girlfriend.
是有關傑克女朋友，瑪姬的事。

B What's your problem?
你腦袋有問題啊？

會話實例

A What's your problem?
你腦袋有問題啊？

B Why? Did I do something wrong?
為什麼這麼說？我有做錯事嗎？

會話實例

A What's your problem?
你腦袋有問題啊？

B Sorry! I didn't mean to.
抱歉，我不是故意的！

我麻煩大了！
I'm in big trouble.

A I'm in big trouble.
我麻煩大了！

B What did you do?
你做了什麼事？

A Idiot. Look what you have done!
笨蛋！看你做的好事！

B Shit. I'm in big trouble.
糟糕！我麻煩大了！

A I'm in trouble now. Can you help me?
我現在有麻煩了，你能幫我嗎？

B Sure, what is it?
好啊，什麼事？

🔊 39

不要管我！
Leave me alone.

會話實例

A You're such a loser.
你真是失敗者！

B Leave me alone.
不要管我！

會話實例

A You're pathetic!
你真是悲哀！

B Leave me alone.
不要管我！

會話實例

A Hey. Stop it.
就是你！住手！

B Just leave us alone.
不要管我們！

你是在自找麻煩啊！
You're asking for trouble.

會話實例

A You're asking for trouble.
你是在自找麻煩。

B Sorry for that.
我為那件事感到抱歉啦！

會話實例

A You're asking for trouble.
你是在自找麻煩。

B Me? I don't think so.
我？我不這麼認為！

會話實例

A Please? Just once?
拜託啦！一次就好？

B You're really asking for trouble.
你真的是在自找麻煩啊！

40

要花好多時間耶！
It takes so much time.

會話實例

A Please?
拜託好嗎？

B It takes so much time.
要花好多時間耶！

會話實例

A Seriously!
我是說真的！

B I know. It takes so much time.
我知道！要花好多時間耶！

會話實例

A It takes so much time.
要花好多時間耶！

B So what? Just do it.
那又如何呢？做就對了！

注意點！
Look out!

A Look out!

注意點！

B Thank you. You saved my life.

謝謝你！你救了我一命！

A Look out!

注意點！

B Shit! What the hell was that?

可惡！那是什麼鬼東西？

A Here comes my bus.

我等的公車來了！

B Look out!

注意點！

41

我來示範給你看！
Let me show you.

會話實例

A I don't know how to turn it on.
我不知道怎麼打開！

B Let me show you.
我來示範給你看！

會話實例

A Let me show you.
我來示範給你看！

B Impressive. I can't believe it.
真是令人印象深刻！我真是不敢相信！

會話實例

A Let me show you. See?
我來示範給你看！懂嗎？

B I see.
我瞭解了！

我們大家都知道！
We all know it.

會話實例

A We're not alone.
我們並不孤單。

B We all know it.
我們大家都知道！

會話實例

A I've tried.
我試過了！

B We all know it.
我們大家都知道！

會話實例

A I have no choice.
我別無選擇！

B We all know it.
我們大家都知道！

🔵 42

我可以幫得上忙嗎？
Can I help?

會話實例

A Can I help?

我可以幫得上忙嗎？

B Thank you, Jack. You're so sweet.

傑克，謝謝你。你真是貼心！

會話實例

A Can I help?

我可以幫得上忙嗎？

B Sure. Pass me the pen.

好啊！把筆遞給我。

會話實例

A Can I help?

我可以幫得上忙嗎？

B No, thanks. I'm fine.

不，謝了！我可以自己處理！

我能做什麼？
What can I do?

會話實例

A Do something different.
做點不一樣的事吧！

B What can I do?
我能做什麼？

會話實例

A What can I do?
我能做什麼？

B Anything!
都可以！

會話實例

A What can I do?
我能做什麼？

B Nothing you can do.
你什麼事都無法做！

● 43

我有聽說了！
I've heard.

會話實例

A He's a weird person.
他真是怪人。

B I've heard.
我有聽說了！

會話實例

A He gotta go away.
他得要離開！

B I've heard.
我有聽說了！

會話實例

A You know what happened to Maggie?
你知道瑪姬發生什麼事了嗎？

B I've heard.
我有聽說了！

我有一個計畫！
I have a plan.

會話實例

A I have a plan.
我有一個計畫！

B What are you gonna do?
你要做什麼？

會話實例

A What can we do now?
我們現在能怎麼辦？

B I have a plan.
我有一個計畫！

會話實例

A Listen, I have a plan.
聽好，我有一個計畫！

B Yes?
是什麼？

44

瞭解！
Got it.

會話實例

A Let me show you.
我示範給你看！

B Got it.
瞭解！

會話實例

A See? It's not so hard.
瞭解嗎？沒有那麼難！

B Got it.
瞭解！

會話實例

A Got it.
瞭解！

B Good. It's your turn now.
很好！現在輪到你了！

我會考慮看看！
I'll think about it.

會話實例

A What do you think?
你覺得呢？

B I'll think about it.
我會考慮看看！

會話實例

A Don't you think it's a good idea?
你不覺得這是個好主意？

B Yeah. I'll think about it.
是啊！我會考慮看看！

會話實例

A I'll think about it.
我會考慮看看！

B Let me know your decision by to-morrow.
明天之前讓我知道你的決定。

45

你有心事喔！
You worry about something.

會話實例

A You worry about something.
你有心事喔！

B No, I am not.
沒有，我沒有啊！

會話實例

A You worry about something.
你有心事喔！

B How would you know?
你怎麼會知道？

會話實例

A You worry about something.
你有心事喔！

B It's about my parents.
是有關我父母的事。

你可以有選擇權！
You have a choice.

會話實例

A I don't know what to do now.
我現在不知道該怎麼辦。

B You have a choice.
你可以有選擇權！

會話實例

A You have a choice.
你可以有選擇權！

B I don't think so.
我不這麼認為！

會話實例

A What shall I do now?
我現在要做什麼？

B You do have a choice.
你的確是有選擇權！

🔵 46

我有試過了。
I've tried.

會話實例

A I've tried.
我有試過了。

B But it didn't work, right?
但是沒有用，對嗎？

會話實例

A I've tried.
我有試過了。

B Then what did they say?
那他們說了什麼？

會話實例

A It's your responsibility.
這是你的責任。

B But I've tried.
但是我有試過。

我泡了些茶給你。
I made some tea for you.

A I made some tea for you.
我泡了些茶給你。

B You're so sweet.
你真貼心！

A I made some tea for you.
我泡了些茶給你。

B Thank you.
謝謝你！

A I made some tea for you.
我泡了些茶給你。

B No, thanks.
我不想喝，謝謝！

47

不是我做的！
I didn't do it.

會話實例

A I didn't do it.
不是我做的！

B We all know it.
我們大家都知道！

會話實例

A How could you...?
你怎麼可以…？

B Not me. I didn't do it.
不是我！不是我做的！

會話實例

A Jack? Did you do it?
傑克？是你做的嗎？

B Me? No, I didn't do it.
我？不是啊！不是我做的！

我們投票決定。
Let's put it to a vote.

會話實例

A No, I don't agree.
不，我不贊成！

B OK. Let's put it to a vote.
好，那我們投票決定。

C I agree.
我同意！

會話實例

A Don't listen to him.
不要聽他的。

B Why not? My opinion is that we should...
為什麼不可以？我的想法是我們應該…

C Be quiet. Let's put it to a vote.
安靜點！我們投票決定。

48

我要去辦點事。
I have to run an errand.

會話實例

A Where are you going?
你要去哪裡？

A I have to run an errand.
我要去辦點事。

會話實例

A Got a minute to talk?
有空聊一聊嗎？

B Sorry. I have to run an errand.
抱歉。我要去辦點事。

會話實例

A I have to run an errand.
我要去辦點事。

B Sure. Go ahead.
好啊，去吧！

我以你為榮！
I'm proud of you.

A I won!
我贏了！

B I'm proud of you.
我以你為榮！

A Check it out. Isn't it good?
你看！很棒吧？

B Oh, my God! I'm so proud of you.
喔，我的天啊！我真的是以你為榮！

A I made it!
這是我做的！

B Cool. I'm really proud of you.
很酷喔！我真的非常以你為榮！

🔘 49

讚喔！
This is good.

會話實例

A This is good.
讚喔！

B You think so?
你真的這樣認為嗎？

會話實例

A Let's go fishing sometime this wee-kend.
這個週末找個時間去釣魚吧！

B This is good.
不錯啊！

會話實例

A Well? How do you like it?
怎麼樣？你喜歡嗎？

B This is good. How did you do it?
讚喔！你怎麼做到的？

我以前就警告過你啊！
I told you before.

會話實例

A Really? I can't believe it.
真的？真不敢相信！

B I told you before.
我以前就警告過你啊！

會話實例

A I told you before.
我以前就警告過你啊！

B I know, but I can't help it.
我知道！但是我情不自禁啊！

會話實例

A I told you before.
我以前就警告過你啊！

B And what? It just happened so fast.
那又如何呢？事情發生得這麼快！

50

我真是不敢相信！
I can't believe it.

會話實例

A I can't believe it.
我真是不敢相信！

B It's awesome, isn't it?
很棒，對吧？

會話實例

A I can't believe it.
我真是不敢相信！

B What? What happened?
什麼事？發生什麼事了？

會話實例

A I just can't believe it.
我就是不敢相信啊！

B See? Remember what I said?
你看吧！記得我說過什麼嗎？

事情都很順利！
Everything's fine.

會話實例

A How is everything?
事情還好嗎？

B Everything's fine.
事情都很順利！

會話實例

A Is everything fine with you?
你都可以嗎？

B Everything's fine. Don't worry about it.
事情都很順利！不用擔心啦！

會話實例

A Everything's fine.
事情都很順利！

B But you look like shit.
可是你看起來糟透了！

🔴 51

不要拘束。
Make yourself at home.

會話實例

Ⓐ Am I late?
我遲到了嗎？

Ⓑ No! Come on in. Make yourself at home.
不會！進來吧！不要拘束。

會話實例

Ⓐ Make yourself at home. Tea or coffee?
不要拘束。要喝茶還是咖啡？

Ⓑ No, thanks.
都不用，謝謝！

會話實例

Ⓐ Mr. Smith?
你是史密斯先生嗎？

Ⓑ Yes. Come in. Make yourself at home.
是的！進來吧！不要拘束！

我和他分手了！
I broke up with him.

A I broke up with him.
我和他分手了！

B Good for you.
對你來說是好事！

A I broke up with Jack.
我和傑克分手了！

B Oh, sorry to hear that. Are you OK?
喔，真是遺憾！你還好嗎？

A How's Maggie?
瑪姬好嗎？

B Who knows? I broke up with her.
誰知道？我和她分手了！

🔊 52

閉嘴！
Shut up!

會話實例

Ⓐ Mom! Jack took my toys.

媽咪！傑克拿我的玩具！

Ⓑ I didn't.

我沒有！

Ⓒ Shut up!

閉嘴！

會話實例

Ⓐ Shut up!

閉嘴！

Ⓑ What? What did you just say to me?

什麼？你剛剛對我說什麼？

現在不行！
Not now!

A Jack, can you do me a favor?
傑克，可以幫我一個忙嗎？

B Not now!
現在不行！

A Got a minute to talk now?
現在有空聊一聊嗎？

B Not now, please.
拜託，不要現在！

A Listen up!
聽我說！

B Not now. I gotta get out of here.
現在不行啦！我得趕緊閃人了！

🔊 53

快一點！
Hurry up!

會話實例

A Hurry up!
　 快一點！

B Easy. We've got plenty of time.
　 不要緊張！我們有的是時間！

會話實例

A What time is it now?
　 現在幾點了？

B It's 10:30 now!
　 現在十點半了！

A OH, my God! Hurry up!
　 喔，我的老天爺啊！快一點！

不全然是！
Not really.

A Are you planning to go to college?
　你有打算要念大學嗎？

B Not really.
　不全然是！

A Is she an actress?
　她是一位女演員嗎？

B Not really.
　不全然是！

A Are you hoping to go to Hong Kong?
　你希望去香港嗎？

B Not really.
　不全然是！

🔊 54

再說吧！
We'll see.

會話實例

A Can I go swimming?
我可以去游泳嗎？

B We'll see.
再說吧！

會話實例

A Can I go to see a movie with Jack?
我可以和傑克去看電影嗎？

B We'll see.
再說吧！

會話實例

A Maybe we shall try it.
也許我們應該試一試！

B We'll see.
再說吧！

想都別想！
Don't even think about it.

A Don't even think about it.
想都別想！

B So what?
那又怎麼樣呢？

A Buddy, can I...
兄弟，我可以…

B Don't even think about it.
想都別想！

A Give it back to me!
還給我吧！

B Don't even think about it.
想都別想！

🔊 55

這是你的東西嗎？
Is this your stuff?

會話實例

A Check this out. Is this your stuff?
你看！這是你的東西嗎？

B Maybe. I'm not so sure.
有可能！我不是很確定！

會話實例

A Is this your stuff?
這是你的東西嗎？

B No! It's hers.
不是！是她的！

會話實例

A Is this your stuff?
這是你的東西嗎？

B Yes, it's mine.
對，是我的！

可能會，也可能不會！
Maybe, maybe not.

會話實例

A You'd recognize that guy, right?
你會認得那傢伙，對嗎？

B Maybe, maybe not.
可能會，也可能不會！

會話實例

A Maybe you can call him for help.
也許你可以打電話給他請求幫忙！

B Maybe, maybe not.
可能會，也可能不會！

會話實例

A Is it OK with you?
你可以嗎？

B Maybe, maybe not. I'm not so sure.
可能可以，也可能不可以！我不是很確定！

🎧 56

你是認真的嗎？
Seriously?

會話實例

A I can do nothing.
我無能為力。

B Seriously?
你是認真的嗎？

會話實例

A Seriously?
你是認真的嗎？

B Of course. Why?
當然啊！幹嘛這麼問？

會話實例

A Seriously?
你是認真的嗎？

B I don't know. I can't tell.
我不知道！我說不上來！

就照我說的去做！
Just do what I said.

會話實例

A Maybe we should get out of here.
也許我們應該要閃人！

B I don't think it's a good idea.
我不覺得是個好主意！

A Just do what I said.
就照我說的去做！

會話實例

A Push the button now.
現在就按下按鈕！

B Right now?
現在就要嗎？

A Just do what I said.
就照我說的去做！

57

你在等人嗎？
Are you expecting someone?

會話實例

A Are you expecting someone?
你在等人嗎？

B Me? No, not at all.
我？沒有啊！

會話實例

A Are you expecting someone?
你在等人嗎？

B Yes, I'm waiting for one of my friends.
有啊，我在等我的一位朋友！

會話實例

A Are you expecting someone?
你在等人嗎？

B None of your business.
不關你的事！

你玩得開心嗎？
Did you have a good time?

會話實例

A Did you have a good time?
你玩得開心嗎？

B Yes, I did.
是啊！我很開心！

會話實例

A Did you have a good time?
你玩得開心嗎？

B No. It's boring.
沒有！好無聊！

會話實例

A Did you have a good time?
你玩得開心嗎？

B Me? You tell me.
我？你說呢？

🔊 58

我正在忙。
I'm in the middle of something.

會話實例

A Are you busy now?
你現在在忙嗎？

B Yes. I'm in the middle of something.
對！我正在忙。

會話實例

A Keeping busy?
在忙嗎？

B Yes. I'm in the middle of something.
對！我正在忙。

會話實例

A I'm in the middle of something.
對！我正在忙。

B Are you kidding?
你開玩笑的吧？

你搞了什麼飛機？
What the hell did you do?

會話實例

A What the hell did you do?
你搞了什麼飛機？

B Nothing.
什麼都沒有！

A Then what is that?
那麼那是什麼？

會話實例

A Check this out.
你看！

B What the hell did you do?
你搞了什麼飛機？

A Don't you think this is cool?
你不覺得很酷嗎？

🔵 59

有發現什麼嗎？
Anything?

會話實例

A Anything?
有發現什麼嗎？

B Yeah! Check this out.
有！你看！

會話實例

A Anything?
有發現什麼嗎？

B No! Nothing special.
沒有啊！沒什麼特別的。

會話實例

A OK, let's see...
好吧，我來看看…

B Anything?
有發現什麼嗎？

A Yeah, this is weird.
是啊，這個很怪！

我人就在這裡啊！
Here I am.

會話實例

A I thought you were gone.
我以為你失蹤了！

B Here I am.
我人就在這裡啊！

會話實例

A Where have you been?
你跑去哪裡了？

B Here I am.
我人就在這裡啊！

會話實例

A Don't leave me. Please!
拜託，不要離開我！

B Hey, here I am.
嘿，我人就在這裡啊！

🔵 60

有問題嗎？
Something wrong?

會話實例

A Something wrong?
　　有問題嗎？

B No, everything is fine.
　　沒有，一切都很好！

A Are you sure? Don't you think it's too risky?
　　你確定？你不覺得太冒險了嗎？

會話實例

A Well, this is not good.
　　唉，這不太好啊！

B Something wrong?
　　有問題嗎？

A Yeah, check it out.
　　是啊！你看！

看你幹的好事！
Look what you did.

會話實例

A Look what you did.
看你幹的好事！

B I'm really sorry.
我真的很抱歉！

會話實例

A Look what you did.
看你幹的好事！

B Not me! I didn't do it. Really!
不是我！我沒做！真的！

會話實例

A Shit.
糟糕！

B What happened?
發生什麼事了？

A Look what you did.
看你幹的好事！

61

我才不在乎呢！
I don't give a shit.

會話實例

A What do you think of it?
你覺得怎麼樣？

B I don't give a shit.
我才不在乎呢！

A You must be kidding.
你一定是玩笑話吧！

會話實例

A I don't give a shit what you think.
你怎麼想我才不在乎呢！

B How could you say that?
你怎麼能這麼說？

A So what?
那又怎麼樣？

你看！
Check this out.

A Did you find anything?
你有找到什麼東西嗎？

B Yeah, check this out.
有啊！你看！

A What was that?
那是什麼鬼東西？

A Check this out.
你看！

B I can't believe it. It's wonderful.
我真是不敢相信！太好了！

A Check this out. See?
你看！瞭解了嗎？

B How could that be?
怎麼可能啊？

🔊 62

這裡連個人影也沒有！
There's nobody here.

會話實例

A Help! Help!
救命啊！救命啊！

B Come on! There's nobody here.
拜託！這裡連個人影也沒有！

會話實例

A Hello? Anybody here?
喂！有人嗎？

B There's nobody here.
這裡連個人影也沒有！

會話實例

A Where is everybody?
人都跑到哪裡去了？

B There's nobody here.
這裡連個人影也沒有！

你有決定權。
You're the decision maker.

會話實例

A I don't know what to do.
我不知道該怎麼辦。

B Come on. You're the decision maker.
得了吧！你有決定權。

會話實例

A You're the decision maker.
你有決定權。

B Me? Well, I don't think so.
我？呃，我可不這麼認為！

會話實例

A Say something.
給點意見吧！

B Hey, you're the decision maker.
喂，是你有決定權啊！

🔊 63

給點意見啊！
Say something.

會話實例

A Well? Say something.
怎麼樣？給點意見啊！

B Good.
不錯！

A That's all?
就這樣？

會話實例

A Well? Hey, say something.
怎麼樣？嘿，給點意見吧！

B I don't know what to say.
我不知道要說什麼。

會話實例

A Well? Hey, say something.
怎麼樣？嘿，給點意見吧！

B Amazing, I guess.
我想這的確令人感到驚訝！

隨便你相不相信！
Believe it or not.

會話實例

A I can't believe what he did to you.
我真是不敢相信他對你所做的事！

B Believe it or not.
隨便你相不相信！

會話實例

A It can't be. It's not true.
不會吧！這不是真的！

B Believe it or not.
隨便你相不相信！

會話實例

A Believe it or not.
隨便你相不相信！

B OK. What shall we do now?
好吧！我們現在要做什麼？

🔊 64

還用你說！
You're telling me.

會話實例

A If you don't get more exercise you'll get fat.

如果你不多做運動，就會變胖。

B You're telling me.

還用你說！

會話實例

A You're going to lose him.

你快要失去他了！

B You're telling me.

還用你說！

會話實例

A It's a trap. Right?

這是個陷阱，對吧？

B You're telling me.

還用你說！

我是對的嗎？
Am I right?

會話實例

A Am I right?
我是對的嗎？

B Well, I don't really know.
呃…我不太知道耶！

會話實例

A The answer is B.
答案是B。

B What makes you think so?
你為什麼會這麼認為？

A Am I right?
我是對的嗎？

B Bingo!
答對了！

65

得了吧！
Come on.

會話實例

A Help!
　救命啊！

B Come on. Nobody would hear you.
　得了吧！沒有人會聽見你的。

會話實例

A Come on, pal, give me your money.
　朋友，得了吧！把你的錢給我！

B What money?
　什麼錢！

會話實例

A Come on! Don't be a loser.
　得了吧！不要當個失敗者！

B Leave me alone.
　不要管我！

他只是個無名小卒！
He's a nobody.

會話實例

A Who is that guy?
那傢伙是誰？

B He's a nobody.
他只是個無名小卒！

會話實例

A He's a nobody.
他只是個無名小卒！

B He must have a name.
他總有名字啊！

會話實例

A Are you seeing someone?
你有交往的對象嗎？

B He's a nobody.
他只是個無名小卒！

66

不然又如何？
Or what?

會話實例

Ⓐ Don't do this.
不要這麼做！

Ⓑ Or what?
不然你想怎麼樣呢？

Ⓐ I'll call the police.
我會報警！

會話實例

Ⓐ He asked me not to tell you.
他叫我不要告訴你。

Ⓑ Or what?
不然又如何？

Ⓐ I don't know. He didn't tell me.
我不知道！他沒告訴我！

我會讓你知道的！
I'll let you know.

會話實例

A What are you going to do?
你打算怎麼做？

B I'll let you know.
我會讓你知道的！

會話實例

A Shall we talk about it?
我們應該談一談嗎？

B Of course. I'll let you know.
當然！我會讓你知道的！

會話實例

A What's your final decision?
你最後的決定是什麼？

B I'll let you know.
我會讓你知道的！

🎧 67

我想想！
Let me see.

會話實例

A Do you know the answer?
你知道答案嗎？

B Let me see.
我想想！

會話實例

A Let me see.
我想想！

B Hurry up. We don't have much time.
快一點！我們沒有太多的時間了！

會話實例

A I'd like to check in. My name is Jack Smith.
我要登記住宿。我的名字是傑克‧史密斯。

B Sure. Let me see.
好的！我看看！

又沒什麼損失！
What can it hurt?

會話實例

A You should stop drinking.
你應該要戒酒。

B What can it hurt?
會有什麼損失嗎？

A You know, it's not good for your health.
你知道的，這對你的健康不好！

會話實例

A I don't think it's a good idea.
我不覺得是個好主意。

B So? What can it hurt?
所以呢？會有什麼損失嗎？

A Fine. It's up to you.
很好！隨便你！

🎧 68

告訴我實情。
Tell me the truth.

會話實例

A Tell me the truth.
告訴我實情。

B I just can't.
我就是辦不到！

會話實例

A I didn't tell anyone else.
我沒有告訴其他人！

B Just tell me the truth.
那就告訴我實情嘛！

會話實例

A You know what?
你知道嗎？

B What? Tell me the truth.
什麼？告訴我實情。

完全沒有。
Nothing at all.

會話實例

A Do you have anything to say?
你有什麼話要說的嗎？

B Nothing at all.
完全沒有。

會話實例

A What? What happened?
怎麼啦？發生什麼事了？

B Nothing at all.
完全沒有事啊！

會話實例

A What the hell did you do?
你搞了什麼飛機？

B Nothing at all.
完全沒有啊！

69

沒事！
Nothing.

會話實例

A Come on! There must be something.
得了吧！一定有問題！

B Nothing.
沒事！

會話實例

A What the hell did you do?
你搞了什麼飛機？

B Nothing. Why?
沒事！為什麼這麼問？

會話實例

A What? What did you see?
什麼？你看見什麼了？

B Nothing.
沒事！

為什麼？
How come?

A Maybe we misunderstood Jack.
也許我們誤會傑克了！

B How come?
為什麼呢？

A We'd better change our plans.
我們最好改變我們的計畫。

B How come?
為什麼呢？

A I hate Jack. Really!
我恨傑克。我說真的！

B How come?
為什麼呢？

🔊 70

你敢怎樣？
You what?

會話實例

A Young girl, are you alone?
小女孩，自己一個人嗎？

B Get out, or I'll kick your ass.
滾開！不然我會揍扁你！

A You what?
你敢怎樣？

會話實例

A I don't wanna go to school.
我不想去上學。

B You what?
你怎樣？

A Just leave me alone.
不要理我！

我們閃人吧!
Let's get out of here.

會話實例

A Help!

救命啊!

B Hey you! Stop it. I'll call the police.

嘿,你們這些人!住手!我要叫警察了!

A Let's get out of here.

我們閃人吧!

會話實例

A What have you done, guys?

各位,你們做了什麼事?

B Nothing.

沒事啊!

C Listen. Maybe we should get out of here.

聽好!也許我們應該要閃人!

🔊 71

就在這裡！
It's over here.

會話實例

A Where is the map?
地圖在哪裡？

B It's over here.
就在這裡！

會話實例

A Did you see my glasses?
你有看見我的眼鏡嗎？

B They're over here. On your desk.
就在這裡！在你的桌上！

會話實例

A It's over here.
就在這裡！

B Where?
在哪裡？

A Over here!
這裡啊！

我不知道！
I have no idea.

A Do you know what happened?
你知道發生什麼事了嗎？

B I have no idea.
我不知道！

A Where is Maggie?
瑪姬人在哪裡？

B I have no idea.
我不知道！

A I have no idea.
我不知道！

B How come?
怎麼會呢？

🎧 72

現在事情都結束了！
It's over now.

會話實例

A What's wrong?
怎麼啦？

B Don't worry about it. It's over now.
別擔心！現在事情都結束了！

會話實例

A It's over now.
現在事情都結束了！

B No, it's not. See?
沒有，並沒有啊！你看吧？

會話實例

A I can't take it anymore.
我再也受不了了！

B Come on, it's all over now.
不要這樣，現在所有的事情都結束了！

那又怎麼樣？
So what?

會話實例

A So there is no one here.
所以這裡沒有人！

B So what?
那又如何呢？

C Don't you think it's a good chance?
你不覺得這是個好機會嗎？

會話實例

A I don't see anything unusual.
我沒看見不尋常的事啊！

B So what?
那又如何呢？

A Nothing.
沒事！

● 73

我們絕交了！
We're not friends anymore.

會話實例

A Friends?
還是朋友吧！

B No, we're not friends anymore.
不是！我們絕交了！

會話實例

A Now, we're not friends anymore.
現在我們絕交了！

B Oh, give me a break, pal.
喔，少來了，伙伴！

會話實例

A We're not friends anymore. Remember?
我們絕交了！記得嗎？

B Hey, how could you say that?
嘿，你怎麼能這麼說？

誰在敲門啊？
Who is it?

會話實例

A Who is it?
　　誰在敲門啊？

B Room service.
　　客房服務！

會話實例

A Who is it?
　　誰在敲門啊？

B It's me, Jack.
　　是我，傑克啦！

會話實例

A Who is it?
　　誰在敲門啊？

B Please open the door.
　　拜託請開門！

🔊 74

(電話中)你是哪一位？
Who is this?

會話實例

A Hello?

喂？

B Who is this?

你是誰？

A This is Jack calling from Japan.

我是從日本打電話過來的傑克。

會話實例

A Hello, Jack.

喂，傑克啊！

B Who is this?

你是誰？

A Oh, sorry, may I speak to Jack?

喔，抱歉，我可以和傑克講電話嗎？

好啊！
Why not?

會話實例

A Wanna go with us?
想和我們一起去嗎？

B Why not.
好啊！

會話實例

A I wanna go skiing. Wanna come with me?
我要去滑雪。你要和我一起去嗎？

B Sure. Why not?
好啊！我很願意。

會話實例

A Can you do me a favor?
可以幫我一個忙嗎？

B Sure. Why not?
好啊！有什麼不可以的！

● 75

為什麼不行？
Why not?

會話實例

A You shouldn't go with Jack.
你不應該和傑克去！

B Why not?
為什麼不行？

會話實例

A May I come in?
我可以進來嗎？

B I don't think so.
不可以！

A Why not?
為什麼不行？

請幫我一個忙。
Please do me a favor.

會話實例

A Please do me a favor.
請幫我一個忙。

B Sorry, I'm in the middle of something.
抱歉，我正在忙。

會話實例

A Do me a favor. Hold this for me.
請幫我一個忙。幫我拿著！

B No problem.
好！

會話實例

A Would you please do me a favor?
你願意幫幫我嗎？

B Sure. What is it?
好啊！什麼事？

🎧 76

> # 我還有一個問題。
> # I have one more question.

會話實例

A Any questions?
有問題嗎？

B Yeah, I have one more question.
有啊！我還有一個問題。

會話實例

A I have one more question.
我還有一個問題。

B Keep going.
說吧！

會話實例

A I have one more question.
我還有一個問題。

B What's your question?
你的問題是什麼？

A It's about my salary.
是有關我的薪水。

你真是會製造麻煩。
You're really a troublemaker.

會話實例

A Sorry for the whole thing.
對所有的事我感到抱歉！

B I know. You're really a troublemaker.
我知道！你真是會製造麻煩。

會話實例

A I need your help.
我需要你的幫忙！

B You're really a troublemaker.
你真是會製造麻煩。

A Please!
拜託啦！

🔵 77

很糟！
It's bad.

會話實例

A How is the weather out there?
外面天氣如何？

B It's bad.
很糟！

會話實例

A How's everything?
事情順利嗎？

B It's bad.
很糟！

會話實例

A It's bad.
很糟！

B What? What happened?
什麼？發生什麼事了？

算了！
Never mind.

會話實例

A I beg your pardon.
你再說一遍。

B Never mind.
算了！

會話實例

A What did just you say?
你剛剛說什麼？

B Never mind.
算了！

會話實例

A You just let her go?
你就這樣讓她走？

B Never mind.
算了！

🔘 78

你說什麼？
Excuse me?

會話實例

A What the hell...
搞什麼…

B Excuse me?
你説什麼？

會話實例

A Shit.
糟糕！

B Excuse me?
你説什麼？

會話實例

A Excuse me?
你説什麼？

B I said call the police.
我說打電話報警！

不用，多謝了！
No, thanks.

會話實例

A Do you want my advice?
你要我的建議嗎？

B No, thanks. I don't need it.
不用，多謝了。我不需要。

會話實例

A Coffee or tea?
要喝咖啡還是茶？

B No, thanks.
不用，多謝了！

會話實例

A I can help you out.
我可以幫你解決困境！

B No, thanks.
不用，多謝了！

🔵 79

好主意！
Good idea!

會話實例

A Say something.
給點建議吧！

B Maybe we can... this way.
也許我們可以…往這個方向！

A Good idea!
好主意！

會話實例

A Shall we?
可以走了嗎？

B Good idea! Let's go.
好主意！走吧。

會話實例

A Let's move on.
我們繼續向前走吧！

B Good idea.
好主意！

給你一個驚喜！
Surprise!

會話實例

A Hello? Anybody home?
喂？有人在家嗎？

B Surprise!
給你一個驚喜！

會話實例

A Wow! What is this for?
哇！這是幹什麼用的？

B Surprise! Happy birthday!
給你一個驚喜！生日快樂！

會話實例

A I can't believe what you did to me.
我真是不敢相信你對我的所做所為。

B Surprise.
想不到吧！

80

是有關什麼？
What's it about?

會話實例

A He told us an exciting story.
他告訴我們一個很刺激的故事。

B What's it about?
有關什麼？

會話實例

A What happened to Jack?
傑克怎麼啦？

B What's it about?
有關什麼？

會話實例

A What's it about?
有關什麼？

B It's about my ex-wife.
是有關我前妻的事。

你瞧！
Look.

會話實例

A Look.
你瞧！

B Who is that cute guy?
那個帥哥是誰啊？

會話實例

A Look.
你瞧！

B What's this?
這是什麼？

A You don't know what it is?
你不知道是什麼？

B Why shall I know?
為什麼我會知道？

81

我清楚了！
I see.

會話實例

A Where is the bank?
銀行在哪裡？

B It's on your right hand side.
在你的右手邊。

A I see. Thank you.
我清楚了！謝謝你。

會話實例

A Let me show you.
我示範給你看！

B I see.
原來如此。

請問一下！
Excuse me.

會話實例

A Excuse me.
請問一下！

B Yes?
請說！

會話實例

A Excuse me. Where can I get a new one?
請問一下！哪裡可以拿到一個新的？

B OK. Here you are.
好的，給你！

會話實例

A Excuse me. Is it taken?
借過！這個位子有人坐嗎？

B No, it's not.
沒有！

● 82

我會揍扁你！
I'll kick your ass.

會話實例

A I'll kick your ass.
我會揍扁你！

B How dare you.
你敢！

會話實例

A Out of my way.
滾遠一點！

B Or what?
你敢怎樣？

A I'll kick your ass.
我會揍扁你！

請稍候。
Wait a moment, please.

會話實例

A May I see the menu?
可以給我看菜單嗎？

B Wait a moment, please.
請稍候。

會話實例

A May I speak to Mr. Smith?
我要和史密斯先生講電話。

B Wait a moment, please.
請稍候。

A Sure.
好的！

🎧 83

我會的。
I will.

會話實例

A Will you call him again, please?

請你再打電話給他，好嗎？

B OK, I will.

好的，我會的。

會話實例

A Will you finish the sales report by Friday?

你星期五前會完成銷售報告嗎？

B Yes, I will.

對，我會的！

會話實例

A Stay where you are.

待在原地不要離開！

B I will.

我會的。

有問題嗎？
Any problems?

A Any problems?
有問題嗎？

B Nope. Everything is fine.
沒事。沒問題。

A Any problems?
有問題嗎？

B Yes, I have one more question.
有，我還有一個問題。

A Any problems?
有問題嗎？

B Yes, when do you want it?
有，你什麼時候要？

● 84

也許改天吧！
Maybe some other time.

會話實例

A Would you like to have dinner with us?

要不要和我們一起吃晚餐？

B Sorry, I have other plans.

抱歉，我有其他計畫。

A That's OK. Maybe some other time.

沒關係。也許改天。

會話實例

A Let me buy you a drink.

我請你喝一杯。

B Maybe some other time.

也許改天吧！

我是很希望去，但是…
I'd love to, but...

會話實例

A Would you like to have dinner with me?

你要和我一起用晚餐嗎？

B I'd love to, but I have another plan.

我很希望去，但是我有其他計畫了。

會話實例

A Do you want to go out for dinner tonight?

今晚要一起出去吃晚餐嗎？

B I'd love to, but I have work to do.

我很希望去，但是我有工作要做。

會話實例

A Would you like to join us?

要加入我們嗎？

B I'd love to, but I can't.

我很希望去，但是不行啦！

85

再見囉！
See you later.

會話實例

A It's too late now. See you later.
太晚了！再見囉！

B Bye.
再見！

會話實例

A Here comes my bus.
我等的公車來了。

B See you later.
再見囉！

會話實例

A See you later.
再見囉！

B OK, good-bye.
好，再見！

只會花一點點的時間。
It'll only take a moment.

會話實例

A Are you free now?
現在有空嗎？

B No. I'm quite busy.
沒空！我很忙！

A Come on, it'll only take a moment.
不要這樣，只會花一點點的時間。

會話實例

A Please do me a favor.
請幫我一個忙。

B Sure. What is it?
好啊！有什麼事？

A Thanks. It'll only take a moment.
謝啦！只會花一點點的時間。

🔊 86

我被搞瘋了。
It drives me crazy.

會話實例

A How's your job?
你的工作好嗎？

B Not so good. It drives me crazy.
不太好！我被搞瘋了。

會話實例

A Don't be so angry, pal.
伙伴，不要這麼生氣。

B But he drove me crazy.
但是他把我搞瘋了。

會話實例

A How is your daughter?
你女兒好嗎？

B Sometimes she drives us crazy.
有時候她會把我們搞瘋。

那是另外一回事。
That's another matter.

會話實例

A Why don't you change your plans?
你怎麼不改變你的計畫呢？

B That's another matter.
那是另外一回事。

會話實例

A Is this what you want?
這就是你想要的嗎？

B No, that's another matter.
不是，那是另外一回事。

會話實例

A It just happened like that!
事情就這麼發生了！

B I know, but that's another matter.
我知道，但那是另外一回事。

87

他放我鴿子了。
He stood me up.

會話實例

A Did you hear what happened to Jack?

你有聽說傑克發生的事了嗎？

B No. He stood me up.

不知道！他放我鴿子了。

會話實例

A Are you OK? You look so angry.

你還好吧？你看起來好生氣。

B Jack stood me up last night.

傑克昨天晚上放我鴿子。

會話實例

A She stood me up.

她放我鴿子了！

B Oh no. Again?

不會吧？又來了？

可以借用你的電話嗎？
May I use your phone?

會話實例

A May I use your phone?
可以借用你的電話嗎？

B Sure, go ahead.
好啊，你用吧！

會話實例

A May I use your phone?
可以借用你的電話嗎？

B It's over there.
電話就在那裡。

● 88

我犯錯了！
I made a mistake.

會話實例

A I made a mistake.
我犯錯了！

B What the hell did you do?
你搞了什麼飛機？

會話實例

A Shit, I made a mistake.
糟糕，我犯錯了！

B That's OK.
沒關係！

會話實例

A Did you do this?
這是你的傑作嗎？

B Sorry, I made a mistake.
抱歉，我犯錯了！

不是你的錯！
It's not your fault.

會話實例

A Sorry. I don't know how this happened.

抱歉！我不知道怎會發生這件事！

B It's not your fault.

不是你的錯！

會話實例

A Sorry about that.

我為那件事感到很抱歉！

B Come on, it's not your fault.

不要這樣，不是你的錯！

會話實例

A It's not your fault.

不是你的錯！

B But I'm sorry. Really.

但是我很抱歉。真的！

🔊 89

把鹽巴遞給我。
Pass me the salt.

會話實例

A Pass me the salt.
把鹽巴遞給我。

B Here you are.
給你。

會話實例

A Pass me the cup.
把杯子遞給我。

B Yeap. Here you are.
好的！給你！

會話實例

A Pass me the form.
把表格遞給我。

B What form?
什麼表格？

我們可以走了嗎？
Shall we?

會話實例

A Shall we?
我們可以走了嗎？

B I'm ready. Let's go.
我準備好了。走吧！

會話實例

A Shall we?
我們可以走了嗎？

B I'm not ready.
我還沒準備好。

會話實例

A Shall we?
我們可以走了嗎？

B Just give me another 10 minutes.
再給我十分鐘的時間。

● 90

這是做什麼用的？
What is this for?

會話實例

A Here you are.
　　給你！

B What is this for?
　　這是做什麼用的？

會話實例

A Wow! What is this for?
　　哇！這是做什麼用的？

B It's your birthday present.
　　是你的生日禮物！

A You remembered my birthday?
　　你記得我的生日？

B Hey, you're my youngest sister.
　　喂，你是我的小妹耶！

都是一樣的。
It's all the same.

會話實例

A It's over now.
事情都結束了！

B It's all the same.
都是一樣的。

會話實例

A It's all the same.
都是一樣的。

B No, it's not. Here I am.
不，不是的。我人在這裡啊！

會話實例

A What do you think of it?
你覺得如何？

B It's all the same to me.
對我來說都是一樣的。

🎧 91

面對它吧！
Face it.

會話實例

A I'm not ready for this.
這件事我還沒準備好。

B Come on, sweetie, face it.
得了吧，親愛的，面對它吧！

會話實例

A It's a serious problem.
這是一個嚴重的問題。

B I know, but you have to face it.
我知道，但你得要面對它！

會話實例

A Face it.
面對它吧！

B I just can't.
我就是辦不到！

有趣喔！
Interesting.

會話實例

A Interesting.
有趣喔！

B Interesting? No, it's terrible!
有趣？不會吧，是可怕！

會話實例

A Maybe we can do it this way.
也許我們可以這麼做！

B Interesting.
有趣喔！

會話實例

A It's interesting.
有趣喔！

B Yeah, I did it on purpose.
是啊！我故意這麼做的！

92

你是開我玩笑的吧？
Are you kidding me?

會話實例

A Have you ever tried bungee jumping?
你有試過高空彈跳嗎？

B Are you kidding me? No, I haven't.
你是開我玩笑的吧？沒有，我沒試過。

會話實例

A Are you kidding me?
你是開我玩笑的吧？

B Come on, it's just a joke.
不要這樣，這只是個笑話！

會話實例

A Are you kidding me?
你是開我玩笑的吧？

B I am serious.
我是認真的。

不會吧！
No kidding.

會話實例

A We were doing wild things all night.
我們一整晚都在作很狂野的事情。

B No kidding.
不會吧！

會話實例

A She is in her birthday suit.
她什麼也沒穿。

B No kidding.
不會吧！

會話實例

A He is gay.
他是(男)同性戀。

B No kidding.
不會吧！

🎧 93

我對打棒球有興趣。
I'm interested in playing baseball.

會話實例

A I'm interested in playing baseball.
我對打棒球有興趣。

B Really? Me too.
真的嗎？我也是。

會話實例

A What do you like to do on the weekend?
你週末喜歡做什麼事？

B I'm interested in reading books.
我對閱讀有興趣。

少來了！
Get out of here.

A I'm gonna ask her out.
我要約她出去。

B Get out of here.
少來了！

A I'm richer than anyone you'll ever meet.
我將會是你見過比任何人都還有錢的人。

B Get out of here.
少來了！

A He's so cute.
他真帥！

B Get out of here.
少來了！

🔊 94

你被禁足了！
You are grounded.

會話實例

Ⓐ You are grounded.
你被禁足了！

Ⓑ It's not fair.
不公平！

Ⓐ Go into your room. Now.
進去你的房間。現在就去！

會話實例

Ⓐ What the hell was that?
那是什麼鬼東西？

Ⓑ Sorry. It won't happen again.
對不起，我保證不會再犯。

Ⓐ You are grounded.
你被禁足了！

真是悲哀！
It's pathetic!

會話實例

A Did you hear what happened to Jack?

你有聽説傑克發生的事了嗎？

B Yeah, it's pathetic!

有啊！真是悲哀！

會話實例

A So I tried not to visit them.

所以我盡量不去拜訪他們。

B Pathetic!

真是悲哀！

會話實例

A You're pathetic, buddy!

兄弟，你真是悲哀！

B Leave me alone.

不要管我！

🔊 95

我無能為力。
I can do nothing.

會話實例

A Don't you do something?
你不挽救嗎？

B I can do nothing.
我無能為力。

A Pathetic!
真是悲哀！

會話實例

A I can do nothing.
我無能為力。

B Cheer up. It's all over now.
高興點，事情都結束了！

我情不自禁啊！
I can't help it.

會話實例

A Just leave her alone.
離她遠一點！

B I can't help it.
我情不自禁啊！

會話實例

A Why don't you just go away?
你為何不就走開呢？

B I can't help it.
我情不自禁啊！

會話實例

A No, don't do this.
不要，不要這麼做！

B But I can't help it.
但是我情不自禁啊！

🔊 96

就這樣嗎？
That's all?

會話實例

A That's all?
就這樣嗎？

B OK, it's impressive!
好吧，的確令人印象深刻！

會話實例

A That's all?
就這樣嗎？

B What else do you expect?
不然你還期望什麼？

會話實例

A It's a long story.
說來話長！

B That's all?
就這樣嗎？

這件事好玩喔！
Funny thing!

會話實例

A Take a look at this.
你看看！

B Funny thing, isn't it
這件事好玩喔，對嗎？

A I just knew it. You like it.
我就知道！你喜歡這個。

會話實例

A Funny thing!
這件事好玩喔！

B I don't think so.
我不這麼認為耶！

A Why not?
為什麼不？

● 97

怎麼啦？
What's wrong?

會話實例

A The game sucks.
這場比賽爛透了！

B Why? What's wrong?
為什麼會呢？怎麼啦？

會話實例

A What's wrong?
怎麼啦？

B Nothing!
沒事！

會話實例

A What's wrong?
怎麼啦？

B Please call me an ambulance.
請幫我叫一輛救護車！

重點是什麼？
What's the point?

會話實例

A Do you know what I'm trying to explain?

你知道我要解釋的意思嗎？

B No. What's the point?

不知道！重點是什麼？

會話實例

A What's the point?

重點是什麼？

B The point is that you have to stop hurting them.

重點是你必須停止傷害他們。

會話實例

A What's the point?

重點是什麼？

B Well, I have no clue.

呃，我不知道耶！

🔘 98

對我來說不是！
Not to me.

會話實例

A Don't you think it's a good chance?
你不覺得這是個好機會嗎？

B Not to me.
對我來說不是！

A Why not?
為什麼不是？

會話實例

A This is a great idea.
好主意！

B Not to me.
對我來說不是！

A What do you mean by that?
你是什麼意思？

你是這麼想的嗎？
This is what you thought?

會話實例

A Funny!
好玩喔！

B Funny? This is what you thought?
好玩？你是這麼想的嗎？

會話實例

A This is cool.
酷喔！

B This is what you thought?
你是這麼想的嗎？

會話實例

A This is what you thought?
你是這麼想的嗎？

B Yeah, why not?
是啊，為什麼不？

🔊 99

對你來說是好事。
Good for you.

會話實例

A There's a chance that I'll see him.
我有一個可以見他的好機會。

B Good for you. Just ask him to believe you.
對你來說是好事。只要要求他能夠相信你。

會話實例

A I should stop smoking.
我應該要戒菸。

B Good for you.
對你來説是好事。

這個由我來幫你。
Let me help you with this.

會話實例

A Let me help you with this.
這個由我來幫你。

B It's very kind of you.
你真好。

會話實例

A Let me help you with this.
這個由我來幫你。

B Thank you so much.
太感謝你了！

會話實例

A Let me help you with this.
這個由我來幫你。

B No, thanks. I can manage it by my-self.
不用了，謝謝！我可以自己處理。

🔊 100

我到家囉！
I am home.

會話實例

A I am home.
我到家囉！

B Surprise! Happy birthday!
給你一個驚喜！生日快樂！

會話實例

A I am home. Hello?
我到家囉！有人在嗎？

B Over here, sweetie.
親愛的，我在這裡。

會話實例

A You are home early.
你今天早提回來。

B I'm tired. I wanna have a bath.
我很累。我想洗個澡。

我不是很有把握！
I'm not so sure.

A Can you recognize this guy?
你可以指認這傢伙嗎？

B I think so, but I'm not so sure.
我是這樣想的，但是我不是很有把握！

A Is this your stuff?
這是你的東西嗎？

B Could be. I'm not so sure.
有可能！我不是很有把握！

A Do you wanna go skiing?
你要去滑雪嗎？

B I'm not so sure.
我不是很確定！

101

我不太清楚。
I don't know for sure.

會話實例

A Where is Jack?
傑克人在哪裡？

B I don't know for sure.
我不太清楚。

會話實例

A Who did this to you?
誰對你做的事？

B I don't know for sure.
我不太清楚。

會話實例

A Do you know how to solve it?
你知道要怎麼解決嗎？

B I don't know for sure.
我不太清楚。

喔，沒什麼啦！
Oh, it's nothing.

會話實例

A Cool, man.

兄弟，酷斃了！

B Oh, it's nothing.

喔，沒什麼啦！

會話實例

A Thank you for the help.

謝謝你的幫助。

B Oh, it's nothing.

喔，沒什麼啦！

會話實例

A Bye. Thanks for the dinner, Jack.

再見，傑克，謝謝你的晚餐喔！

B Oh, it's nothing. Really.

喔，沒什麼啦！真的！

● 102

酷斃了！
Cool!

會話實例

A What do you think of it?
你覺得怎麼樣？

B Cool!
酷斃了！

會話實例

A See? Isn't it great?
你瞧，不是很棒嗎？

B Cool.
酷斃了！

會話實例

A This is cool.
酷斃了！

B Oh, it's nothing.
喔，沒什麼啦！

快一點！
Hurry up.

A Hurry up.
快一點！

B I can't walk any longer.
我不能再走了。

A There are few minutes left.
沒有幾分鐘了。

B OK, hurry up.
好，快一點！

A Hurry up. We're late.
快一點！我們遲到了。

B It's still early.
還很早！

🔊 103

說來話長。
It's a long story.

會話實例

A What the hell are you doing here?
你在這裡搞什麼？

B It's a long story.
說來話長。

會話實例

A What happened to you?
你們發生什麼事了？

B It's a long story.
說來話長。

會話實例

A It's a long story.
說來話長。

B Try me.
說來聽聽！

你是他們的一份子嗎？
Are you one of them?

會話實例

A Are you one of them?
你是他們的一份子嗎？

B What do you say?
你說呢？

會話實例

A Who are you?
你是誰？

B I'm one of them.
我是他們的一份子。

會話實例

A Who is that tall guy?
那個高個子的傢伙是誰？

B It's Jack. He's one of them.
是傑克。他是他們的一份子。

🔊 104

我們有五個人。
There are five of us.

會話實例

A I'd like to make a reservation.
我要預約座位。

B How many, please?
請問有多少人？

A There are five of us.
我們有五個人。

會話實例

A How many of you have ever seen it?
你們有多少人看過？

B There are only three of us.
我們只有三個人看過。

你提早到了。
You're early.

會話實例

A I'd like to see Mr. Jones.
我要見瓊斯先生。

B You're early.
你早到了。

會話實例

A I am home.
我到家囉！

B You're early.
你提早到了。

會話實例

A Sorry, I'm late.
抱歉，我遲到了！

B No, you're early.
不會，你是提早到了。

🔊 105

你真的不在意，對吧？
You really don't care, do you?

會話實例

A I don't wanna see you anymore.
我不想再見到你了！

B You really don't care, do you?
你真的不在意，對吧？

會話實例

A You really don't care, do you?
你真的不在意，對吧？

B Not now. It's a long story.
現在不要談！説來話長！

會話實例

A You really don't care, do you?
你真的不在意，對吧？

B Oh, baby, what made you think so?
喔！親愛的！你怎麼會這麼認為呢？

我很在乎你！
I care about you a lot.

會話實例

A Do you still love me?
你還愛我嗎？

B I care about you a lot.
我很在乎你！

會話實例

A I care about you a lot.
我很在乎你！

B Then don't leave me.
那就不要離開我。

會話實例

A I care about you a lot.
我很在乎你！

B Don't! I can't take it anymore.
不要說了！我受不了了！

🔴 106

你覺得呢？
Well?

會話實例

A Well?
你覺得呢？

B It sucks.
糟透了！

會話實例

A Come on, what happened?
怎麼啦？發生什麼事了？

B Check it out. Well?
你看！你覺得呢？

A My God. It's pathetic!
我的天啊！真是悲哀！

太好了！
Yes!

A You know what? He made it.
你知道嗎？他辦到了！

B Yes!
太好了！

A You are the winner.
你是冠軍！

B Yes!
太好了！

A Here you are.
給你！

B Yes! I just knew it.
太好了！我就是知道！

107

真是遺憾聽見你這麼說。
I'm sorry to hear that.

會話實例

A I broke up with Jack.
我和傑克分手了！

B I'm sorry to hear that.
真是遺憾聽見你這麼説。

會話實例

A It sucks.
糟透了！

B Oh, I'm sorry to hear that.
喔，真是遺憾聽見你這麼説。

會話實例

A We failed.
我們失敗了！

B Sorry to hear that.
真是遺憾聽見你這麼説。

我就知道！
I just knew it.

會話實例

A See? We're not alone here.
看吧？我們並不孤單！

B I just knew it.
我就知道！

會話實例

A Check it out. Isn't it great?
你看！很棒吧？

B Excellent. I just knew it.
太好了！我就知道！

會話實例

A We all know that.
這是我們大家都知道的事！

B I knew it.
我就知道！

🔘 108

是啊，我知道啦！
Yeah, I know.

會話實例

Ⓐ They are coming for you!

他們來找你了！

Ⓑ Yeah, I know.

是啊，我知道啦！

會話實例

Ⓐ He shouldn't have done it.

他不應該這麼做！

Ⓑ Yeah, I know.

是啊，我知道啦！

會話實例

Ⓐ Stay put, OK?

不要動，好嗎？

Ⓑ Yeah, I know.

好啦，我知道啦！

你可以嗎？
Is it OK with you?

會話實例

A You mean we have to wait?
你是說我們必須要等囉？

B Is it OK with you?
你可以嗎？

A Sure, why not?
好啊，為什麼不可以？

會話實例

A Is it OK with you?
你可以嗎？

B Yeah, it's OK.
是啊！沒問題！

會話實例

A Is it OK with you?
你可以嗎？

B Me? I don't think so.
你問我？我不這麼認為！

🔵 109

你看起來臉色蒼白。
You look pale.

會話實例

A You look pale.
你看起來臉色蒼白。

B I'm not feeling well.
我覺得不舒服。

A Do you want me to call an ambulance?
你要我叫救護車嗎？

B Please do.
麻煩你囉！

會話實例

A You look pale. Are you OK?
你看起來臉色蒼白。你還好嗎？

B Terrible, I guess.
我想很糟糕吧！

什麼事？
What's up?

會話實例

A Do me a favor, OK?
幫我一個忙，好嗎？

B Sure. What's up?
好啊！什麼事？

會話實例

A Hey.
就是你！

B What's up?
什麼事？

會話實例

A Hey, what's up?
嘿，近來有什麼事嗎？

B Well, I have news for you.
是這樣的，我有事情要告訴你。

🔘 110

我就是！
It's me.

會話實例

A Next, please. Mr. Smith?
麻煩下一位！史密斯先生嗎？

B It's me.
我就是！

會話實例

A Hey, you!
就是你！

B Yes?
有事嗎？

A Are you Jack Jones?
你是傑克‧瓊斯嗎？

B Yes, it's me.
是的，我就是！

不用放心上！
It's OK.

會話實例

A Sorry.
抱歉！

B It's OK.
不用放心上！

會話實例

A Sorry about that.
那件事我很抱歉！

B It's OK.
不用放心上！

會話實例

A Thank you so much.
非常感謝你！

B It's OK.
不用放心上！

● 111

不用擔心啦！
Don't worry about it.

會話實例

A It's terrible.
太可怕了！

B Don't worry about it.
不用擔心啦！

會話實例

A I promise that I can do it better next time.
我保證下一次我可以做得更好！

B Don't worry about it.
不用擔心啦！

會話實例

A Where is Maggie?
瑪姬人在哪裡？

B Don't worry about her.
不用擔心她啦！

我為那件事感到很抱歉！
Sorry about that.

會話實例

A See? I told you before.
我就説嘛！我以前就警告過你！

B I know. Sorry about that.
我知道！我為那件事感到很抱歉！

會話實例

A Sorry about that.
我為那件事感到很抱歉！

B No, not at all.
不會啦！

會話實例

A I'm sorry about that.
我為那件事感到很抱歉！

B It's not your fault.
不是你的錯啦！

🔊 112

那件事我厭煩了！
I'm tired of it.

會話實例

A What would you say?
你認為呢？

B I'm tired of it.
對那件事我厭煩了！

會話實例

A I'm tired of it.
對那件事我厭煩了！

B Come on, you can make it.
不要這樣，你可以辦得到的。

會話實例

A She always talks about her new boy-friend.
她老是談論她的新男友。

B I'm tired of hearing it.
那件事我聽膩了。

你怎麼能這麼說？
How could you say that?

會話實例

A You know what? I'm sick of you.
你知道嗎？我對你厭煩了。

B How could you say that?
你怎麼能這麼說？

會話實例

A He's nobody.
他是個無名小卒。

B How could you say that?
你怎麼能這麼說？

會話實例

A Everybody calm down.
大家都冷靜點！

B Calm down? How could you say that?
冷靜？你怎麼能這麼說？

🔘 113

不要再這麼說了！
Don't say that again.

會話實例

A I give up.
我放棄了！

B Don't say that again.
不要再這麼說了！

會話實例

A I don't wanna see him anymore.
我不要再看見他了！

B Don't ever say that again.
永遠不要再這麼說了！

會話實例

A I'm really sorry.
我真的很抱歉！

B Hey, don't say that again.
嘿，不要再這麼說了！

多謝啦！
Thanks a lot.

會話實例

A Thanks a lot.
多謝啦！

B My pleasure.
（能幫助你）是我的榮幸！

會話實例

A If you need any help, just let me know.
如果你需要任何的幫助，告訴我一聲。

B Thanks a lot.
多謝啦！

會話實例

A Thanks a lot.
多謝啦！

B You're welcome.
不客氣！

114

都是你造成的！
Thanks to you.

會話實例

A What a mess here.
這裡真是亂啊！

B I didn't mean it.
我不是故意的！

A Thanks to you.
都是你造成的！

會話實例

A You are mad at me, aren't you?
你很氣我，對嗎？

B Yeah, thanks to you.
是啊，都是你造成的！

A I said I'm sorry.
我說了對不起嘛！

需要我幫忙嗎？
May I help you?

會話實例

A May I help you?
需要我幫忙嗎？

B Yes. May I take a look at it?
是的。我可以看一下嗎？

會話實例

A May I help you?
需要我幫忙嗎？

B No, thanks. I can manage it by my-self.
不用，謝謝！我可以自己處理。

會話實例

A Excuse me.
請問一下！

B Yes. May I help you?
好的！需要我幫忙嗎？

115

不客氣！
Anytime.

會話實例

A Thank you so much.
非常感謝你！

B Anytime.
不客氣！

會話實例

A Thanks! It's not easy for you.
謝謝！對你來說真不簡單！

B Anytime.
不客氣！

他正忙線中。
He's on another line.

會話實例

A May I speak to Jack?
我可以和傑克講電話嗎？

B I'm sorry, but he's on another line.
抱歉，但是他正忙線中。

會話實例

A Is Jack around?
傑克在嗎？

B He's on another line.
他正忙線中。

會話實例

A Jack is on another line.
傑克正忙線中。

B I see. May I leave a message?
瞭解！我可以留言嗎？

🔵 116

我可以進來嗎？
May I come in?

會話實例

A May I come in?
我可以進來嗎？

B Sure, come on in.
好的，請進來！

會話實例

A May I come in?
我可以進來嗎？

B No, I don't think so.
不，不可以！

會話實例

A Mrs. Jones? May I come in?
瓊斯太太嗎？我可以進來嗎？

B May I see your badge?
給我看你的證件。

你做給我看。
You show me.

會話實例

A There are other ways to do this exercise.

還可以用別的方法做這個練習。

B You show me.

你做給我看。

會話實例

A I can lift it by myself.

我可以自己舉起來！

B Show me.

表演給我看啊！

會話實例

A You show me.

你做給我看。

B No problem.

好啊！

🔵 117

免談！
No way.

會話實例

A Will you lend me your car?
你車借給我好嗎？

B No way.
免談！

會話實例

A Can I have a dog?
我可以養狗嗎？

B No way.
免談！

會話實例

A I wanna go shopping with Maggie.
我想和瑪姬去逛街！

B No way.
免談！

交給我就對了！
Just leave it to me.

會話實例

A I'll talk to him.
我會和他談一談。

B Don't worry. Just leave it to me.
不用擔心！交給我就對了！

會話實例

A What are you gonna do?
你打算怎麼處理？

B Just leave it to me.
交給我就對了！

會話實例

A Just leave it to me.
交給我就對了！

B To you? No, I don't think so.
交給你？不行，我不這麼認為！

🔘 118

麻煩你了！
Please.

會話實例

A Do you wanna see the menu?
你要看菜單嗎？

B Yes, please.
麻煩你了！

會話實例

A May I help you?
需要我幫忙嗎？

B Please. I'd like to make a reservation.
麻煩你了！我要預約座位。

會話實例

A Tea?
要喝茶嗎？

B Yes, please.
好的，麻煩你了！

你呢？
You?

會話實例

A Hi, how are you doing?
嗨，你好嗎？

B Good. You?
很好！你呢？

會話實例

A Which one do you want?
你想要哪一個？

B The red one.
紅色的這個。

A Good. You?
很好！你呢？

C No, thanks.
我不用，謝了！

🎧 119

我好傷心。
I felt sad.

會話實例

A Are you OK?
你還好嗎？

B I felt sad.
我覺得傷心。

會話實例

A I felt sad.
我覺得傷心。

B What's wrong? It's about John again?
怎麼啦？又是有關約翰嗎？

A Yeah.
是啊！

B Don't worry. He just needs time.
不用擔心！他只是需要時間。

冷靜一點！
Calm down.

會話實例

A Everybody calm down.
大家都冷靜點！

B WHAT? It's too late now.
什麼嘛！太晚了！

會話實例

A Where is the money?
錢在哪裡？

B Easy! Calm down.
不要緊張！冷靜一點！

會話實例

A Just calm down, madam.
女士，冷靜一點！

B I just can't.
我就是辦不到！

🔊 120

你好嗎？
How are you doing?

會話實例

A Hello, how are you doing?
哈囉，你好嗎？

B Great. And you?
很好！你好嗎？

會話實例

A Hi.
你好！

B Hello, how are you doing?
哈囉，你好嗎？

會話實例

A How are you doing?
你好嗎？

B Fine. How about you?
不錯！你呢？好嗎？

有人在嗎？
Anybody here?

A Anybody here?
　有人在嗎？

B May I help you?
　需要我幫忙嗎？

A Yes, I need to use the phone.
　是的，我需要打電話。

A Hello? Anybody here?
　喂！有人在嗎？

B Yes?
　有事嗎？

A Thank God. Someone is after me.
　感謝老天爺！有人在追我！

🔵 121

很好！
Great.

會話實例

A What do you think of my idea?
你覺得我的主意怎麼樣？

B Great.
很好！

會話實例

A We can deliver it to you tomorrow morning.
我們明天早上可以送貨給你。

B Great.
很好！

會話實例

A How are you doing?
你好嗎？

B Great.
我很好！

很棒吧？
Isn't it good?

會話實例

A Check it out. Isn't it good?
你看！很棒吧？

B This is great.
很好！

會話實例

A Isn't it good?
很棒吧？

B It's brilliant.
簡直太好了！

會話實例

A Isn't it good?
很棒吧？

B Are you kidding me? It's terrible.
你是開我玩笑的吧？很糟糕耶！

🔘 122

我會和他談一談。
I'll talk to him.

會話實例

A I'll talk to him.
我會和他談一談。

B Are you sure?
你確定嗎？

會話實例

A I'll talk to her.
我會和她談一談。

B About what?
談什麼？

會話實例

A What about my parents?
我父母怎麼辦？

B Don't worry about it. I'll talk to them.
不用擔心啦！我會和他們談一談。

有人在嗎？
Hello?

會話實例

A Hello?

　　有人在嗎？

B Susan! What are you doing here?

　　蘇珊！妳怎麼會在這裡？

會話實例

A Hello?

　　有人在嗎？

B What can I do for you, sir?

　　先生，有什麼需要我效勞的嗎？

會話實例

A Excuse me? Hello?

　　請問一下！有人在嗎？

B Yeah?

　　有事嗎？

🔊 123

我應該怎麼辦？
What shall I do?

會話實例

A You can't do it this way.
你不應該這樣做。

B What shall I do?
我應該怎麼辦？

會話實例

A What shall I do?
我應該怎麼辦？

B You have to try it once more.
你應該再試一次。

會話實例

A What shall I do now?
我現在應該怎麼辦？

B You gotta tell him the truth.
你應該告訴他實話。

送你！
It's for you.

A What is this?
這是什麼？

B It's for you. Happy birthday!
送你！生日快樂！

A It's for you.
送你！

B What for?
為什麼？

A It's for you.
送你！

B Thank you so much.
非常感謝你！

🎧 124

我看看！
Let me take a look.

會話實例

A You gotta fix it.
你得要修好啦！

B Let me take a look.
我看看！

會話實例

A Let me take a look.
我看看！

B Come on, it's not serious.
不用啦！一點都不嚴重！

會話實例

A It's awesome.
太棒了！

B Really? Let me take a look.
真的嗎？我看看！

你在發抖耶！
You're shaking.

會話實例

A Are you OK? You're shaking.
你還好嗎？你在發抖耶！

B I'm not feeling well.
我覺得不舒服。

會話實例

A Hey, you're shaking.
嘿，你在發抖耶！

B I feel so cold.
我覺得好冷。

會話實例

A Hey, you're shaking.
嘿，你在發抖耶！

B I'm afraid of the dark.
我怕黑。

🔊 125

你走錯路了。
You took the wrong way.

會話實例

A Where is the post office?
郵局在哪裡？

B You took the wrong way.
你走錯路了。

會話實例

A Is this the right way to the beach?
去海灘是走這條路嗎？

B No. You took the wrong way.
不是！你走錯路了。

會話實例

A Excuse me. I'm going to the library.
請問一下，我要去圖書館。

B OH, you took the wrong way.
喔，你走錯路了。

你現在有空嗎？
Are you free now?

A Are you free now?
你現在有空嗎？

B Yes. What's up?
有啊！什麼事？

A Are you free now?
你現在有空嗎？

B It depends.
看情況而定。

A Are you free now?
你現在有空嗎？

B No, I'm quite busy now.
沒有，我現在很忙！

🔊 126

在忙什麼？
Busy with what?

會話實例

A Got a minute to talk?
有空聊一聊嗎？

B No, I'm in the middle of something.
沒有，我正在忙！

A Busy with what?
在忙什麼？

會話實例

A I'm busy now.
我現在在忙。

B Busy with what?
在忙什麼？

會話實例

A Busy with what?
在忙什麼？

B Nothing important. What's up?
沒什麼重要的事。什麼事？

真的很划算。
It's a real bargain.

會話實例

A How much is it?
這個賣多少錢？

B It's five hundred dollars.
五百元！

A Not expensive.
不貴嘛！

B It's a real bargain.
真的很划算。

A OK, I'll take it.
好，我要買！

🔊 127

你可以辦得到的。
You can make it.

會話實例

A I don't know what to do.
我不知道該怎麼辦。

B Come on, you can make it.
不要這樣，你可以辦得到的。

會話實例

A You can make it.
你可以辦得到的。

B I just can't.
我就是辦不到！

會話實例

A You can make it.
你可以辦得到的。

B Really? You really think so?
真的嗎？你真這麼認為？

聽起來不錯。
Sounds good.

會話實例

A Would you like to join us?
要加入我們嗎？

B Sounds great.
聽起來不錯。

會話實例

A What do you think of my idea?
你覺得我的想法如何？

B Sounds good.
聽起來不錯。

會話實例

A Let's take a break.
我們休息一下吧！

B Sounds good.
聽起來不錯。

🔊 128

我人在附近。
I was in the neighborhood.

會話實例

A Jack? What are you doing here?
傑克？你在這裡做什麼？

B I was in the neighborhood.
我人在附近。

A Come on in. Make yourself at home.
進來吧！不要拘束。

會話實例

A Where were you at that time?
當時候你人在哪裡？

B I was in the neighborhood.
我人在附近。

該走囉！
Time to go.

會話實例

A Time to go.
該走囉！

B OK. See you soon.
好！再見！

會話實例

A Time to go.
該走囉！

B I'm not ready yet.
我還沒準備好。

會話實例

A Time to go.
該走囉！

B Good idea! Let's go.
好主意！走吧。

🔵 129

我想你是對的。
I suppose you're right.

會話實例

A Why don't you face it?
你何不面對這個事實？

B I suppose you're right.
我想你是對的。

會話實例

A What would you say?
你認為呢？

B I suppose you're right.
我想你是對的。

會話實例

A It's a trap.
這是陷阱！

B I suppose you're right.
我想你是對的。

我挺你！
I got your back.

會話實例

A What would you say?
你認為呢？

B I got your back.
我挺你！

會話實例

A I got your back.
我挺你！

B Good. Let's move.
太好了！我們行動吧！

會話實例

A I got your back.
我挺你！

B You mean it?
你是認真的嗎？

🔊 130

這是一項簡單的工作。
It's an easy job.

會話實例

A It's too difficult.
這太難了！

B Come on, it's an easy job.
不要這樣嘛，這是一項簡單的工作。

會話實例

A It's an easy job.
這是一項簡單的工作。

B Not for me.
對我來說不是。

會話實例

A It's an easy job. Really.
這是一項簡單的工作。真的！

B Good to hear that.
真高興聽到你這麼說。

就在剛才！
Just now!

會話實例

A When did you find it?
你什麼時候發現的？

B Just now!
就在剛才！

會話實例

A When did they arrive in Taipei?
他們什麼時候抵達台北的？

B Just now!
就在剛才！

會話實例

A When did you come back?
你什麼時候回來的？

B Just now!
剛才才回來的！

131

不要這樣看我！
Don't look at me like that.

會話實例

A It's me.
是我！

B You? I can't believe it.
是你？我真是不敢相信！

A Don't look at me like that.
不要這樣看我！

會話實例

A Don't look at me like that.
不要這樣看我！

B Or what?
不然你想怎樣？

會話實例

A Don't ever look at me like that.
不要再這樣看我了！

B Sorry, it won't happen again.
抱歉！我不會再犯了！

我說的是實話。
I was saying the truth.

會話實例

A Liar.
你說謊！

B I was saying the truth.
我說的是實話。

會話實例

A It can't be.
不可能！

B I was saying the truth.
我說的是實話。

會話實例

A I was saying the truth. Really!
我說的是實話。真的啦！

B Well, perhaps.
嗯，可能是吧！

🔊 132

例如什麼？
Like what?

會話實例

A What would you like to have?
你想喝什麼？

B Like what?
例如什麼？

A Like a cup of tea?
要不要喝杯茶？

B Sounds great.
好主意！

會話實例

A I'll try another way.
我會試試其他方法。

B Like what?
例如什麼？

你有在聽我說話嗎？
Are you listening to me?

會話實例

A Are you listening to me?
你有在聽我說話嗎？

B What? Sorry.
什麼？抱歉！

會話實例

A Are you listening to me?
你有在聽我說話嗎？

B Yes. I have one more question.
有啊！我還有一個問題。

會話實例

A Are you listening to me?
你有在聽我說話嗎？

B Excuse me?
你說什麼？

🔊 133

我請你喝一杯吧！
Let me buy you a drink.

會話實例

A Jack! Good to see you!
傑克！真高興見到你！

B Me, too. Let me buy you a drink.
我也是。我請你喝一杯吧！

會話實例

A Let me buy you a drink.
我請你喝一杯。

B Maybe some other time.
也許改天吧！

會話實例

A Let me buy you a drink.
我請你喝一杯。

B So kind of you.
你真好！

不要再這麼說了！
Don't ever say that again.

會話實例

A Sucks!
糟透了！

B Don't ever say that again.
不要再這麼説了！

會話實例

A I don't wanna see you anymore.
我不想再見到你了！

B Don't ever say that again.
不要再這麼説了！

會話實例

A Don't ever say that again.
不要再這麼説了！

B Fine.
好！

● 134

坐吧！
Take a seat.

會話實例

A Madam, please come in.
女士，請進！

B Please. Just call me Maggie.
拜託，叫我瑪姬就好！

A OK. Maggie. Take a seat.
好吧！瑪姬！坐吧！

會話實例

A Take a seat. What would you like to have?
坐吧！你想吃點什麼？

B Water would be fine.
喝水就好！

跟我來！
Follow me.

A Follow me.
跟我來！

B Sure.
好！

A Follow me. Watch your step.
跟我來！小心腳步！

B I will.
我會的！

A Gentlemen, please follow me.
各位先生，請跟我來！

B Sure. Thank you.
好！謝謝！

🔊 135

誰是這裡的主管？
Who's in charge here?

會話實例

A How may I help you?
需要我協助嗎？

B Who's in charge here?
誰是這裡的主管？

會話實例

A Who's in charge here?
誰是這裡的主管？

B It's me.
是我！

會話實例

A Who's in charge here?
誰是這裡的主管？

B It's Jack. He's over there.
是傑克。他在那裡。

不要緊張！
Take it easy.

會話實例

A Somebody help me.
誰來救救我啊！

B Take it easy, madam.
女士，不要緊張！

會話實例

A Don't get any closer.
不要再靠近！

B Take it easy.
不要緊張！

會話實例

A Take it easy, man.
兄弟，不要緊張！

B I just can't.
我就是辦不到！

🔊 136

想想辦法啊！
Do something.

會話實例

A Do something.
想想辦法啊！

B I'm trying.
我正在想辦法啊！

會話實例

A Do something.
想想辦法啊！

B What shall I do?
我該怎麼辦？

會話實例

A Do something.
想想辦法啊！

B I have an idea.
我有一個主意。

深呼吸！
Take a deep breath.

會話實例

A Help!

　救命啊！

B Calm down. Take a deep breath.

　冷靜點！深呼吸！

會話實例

A Take a deep breath.

　深呼吸！

B I just can't. I can't breathe.

　我就是辦不到！我不能呼吸了！

會話實例

A Take a deep breath.

　深呼吸！

B Go away. Leave me alone.

　走開！你不要管我！

🔊 137

目前為止都還好。
So far so good.

會話實例

A How is everything?
你好嗎？

B So far so good.
目前為止都還好。

會話實例

A Is everything OK?
凡事還好吧？

B So far so good.
目前為止都還好。

會話實例

A So far so good.
目前為止都還好。

B Something's wrong.
有問題喔！

你也是啊！
You too.

會話實例

A Hi, Jack.

嗨，傑克！

B You look great.

你看起來氣色不錯！

A You too.

你也是啊！

會話實例

A Merry Christmas.

耶誕快樂！

B You too.

你也是啊！

會話實例

A Have a nice day.

祝你今天順利！

B You too.

你也要啊！

🔘 138

沒什麼特別的。
Nothing special.

會話實例

A Something wrong?
有事嗎？

B Nothing special.
沒什麼特別的。

會話實例

A Anything new?
有什麼新發現嗎？

B Nothing special.
沒什麼特別的。

會話實例

A How is everything?
一切都好嗎？

B Nothing special.
沒什麼特別的。

你知道嗎？
You know what?

會話實例

A You know what?
你知道嗎？

B What? What happened?
什麼？發生什麼事了？

會話實例

A Are you OK?
你還好嗎？

B You know what? I broke up with Maggie.
你知道嗎？我和瑪姬分手了！

C Sorry to hear that.
真是遺憾！

🔊 139

我願意！
I'd love to.

會話實例

A Would you like to come to my party?

要不要來參加我的派對？

B I'd love to.

我願意！

會話實例

A Would you like to hang out with us?

要和我們出去嗎？

B I'd love to.

我願意！

會話實例

A What would you like to drink? Tea?

你想喝什麼？茶好嗎？

B I'd love to.

好！

祝好運！
Good luck.

A Good luck.
祝好運！

B OK. Bye.
好，再見！

A Good luck.
祝好運！

B You too. See you later.
你也是！再見！

A Good luck.
祝好運！

B I really need it.
我真的很需要好運！

🔘 140

滾開！
Get lost.

會話實例

A Let me help you.
讓我來幫你！

B Get lost.
滾開！

會話實例

A Is this what you want?
這就是你想要的？

B Get lost. Leave me alone.
滾開！你不要管我！

會話實例

A Get lost.
滾開！

B Fine. I'll never forgive you!
好！我永遠都不會饒恕你！

慢慢來！
Take your time.

A It's too late now. Gotta go now.
現在太晚了！現在得走了！

B Take your time.
慢慢來！

A I've ruined everything.
我搞砸了一切！

B Take your time.
慢慢來！

A I can't believe what happened.
我不敢相信所發生的事！

B It's OK. Take your time.
沒關係！慢慢來！

🎧 141

算了！
Forget it.

會話實例

A But this is your job.
但這是你的工作啊！

B Forget it.
算了！

會話實例

A What shall I do?
我該怎麼辦？

B Forget it.
算了！

會話實例

A Can you help me?
你可以幫我嗎？

B No way. What's up?
不行！有什麼事？

A Forget it.
算了！

www.foreverbooks.com.tw

永續圖書 線上購物網

超值優惠：　我們家的書，你在這裡都買得到！

這句日語你用對了嗎

擺脫中文思考的日文學習方式

列舉台灣人學日文最常混淆的各種用法

讓你用「對」的日文順利溝通

日本人都習慣這麼說

學了好久的日語，卻不知道…

梳頭髮該用哪個動詞？延長線應該怎麼說？

黏呼呼是哪個單字？當耳邊風該怎麼講？

快翻開這本書，原來日本人都習慣這麼說！

驚喜無限！

不定期推出優惠特賣

永續圖書總代理：專業圖書發行、書局經銷、圖書出版

電話：(886)-2-8647-3663 傳真：(886)-2-86473660

服務信箱：yungjiuh@ms45.hinet.net

五觀藝術出版社、培育文化、棋茵出版社、達觀出版社、可道書
坊、白橡文化、大拓文化、讀品文化、雅典文化、手藝家出版社、
檢書堂、葛蘭絲、智品圖書…………

1000 基礎實用單字（25 開）

想學好英文？就從「單字」下手！
超實用單字全集，簡單、好記、最實用，
讓你打好學習英文的基礎！

旅遊英語萬用手冊（48 開）

想出國自助旅遊嗎？
不論是 出境、入境、住宿，或是 觀光、交通、解決三餐，
通通可以自己一手包辦的「旅遊萬用手冊」！

How do you do 最實用的生活英語（50 開）

史上超強！超好用、超好記、最道地的英文生活用語
讓您一次過足說英語的癮！

遊學必備 1500 句（25 開）

【租屋的訊息】
在人生地不熟的美國，一定要養成主動詢問的習慣，租屋訊息不但可以請教同學，也可以到學校的公佈欄尋找！
Q.1 Can I rent a room for two months?
房間我可以只租兩個月嗎？

超實用商業英文 E-mail
（25 開）

辦公室事務、秘書溝通、商業活動
輕輕鬆鬆十分鐘搞定一封 e-mail

生活句型萬用手冊（48 開）

生活英文萬用手冊，一句短語，就可以和外籍朋
友溝通。

商務英文 E-mail（25 開）

商用 e-mail 撰寫指南，分段解析、標示重
點、範例說明，輕鬆完成每一封 e-mail。E-
mail 寫作不必大作文章，掌握「快、狠、
準」的原則，就可以在最短的時間內完成一
封商用 e-mail…

超有趣的英文基礎文法
（25 開）

最適合國人學習的英文文法書，針對最容
易犯的文法錯誤，解析文法。利用幽默的
筆法，分析看似艱澀的文法，讓文法變得
簡單有趣。淺顯易懂的解說，才是學習英
語文法的王道！

電話英語一本通(附 MP3)
（50 開）

一次搞定所有的英語電話用語！接到外國人的電話，不再結結巴巴！情境式對話，完全不用死背英語！1.打電話找人 2.接電話 3.代接電話 4.轉接電話 5.電話留言讓您不用思考，就能脫口說英語！

商業英文 E-mail 談判篇
（25 開）

你有寫 e-mail 的煩惱嗎？五大句型，讓你輕輕鬆鬆搞定 e-mail！

五大句型，寫 e-mail 真輕鬆：Chapter 1 寫信 Chapter 2 通知 Chapter 3 請求 Chapter 4 抗議 Chapter 5 建議

我的菜英文【工作職場篇】
（25 開）

超強職場英語 一次收錄/警察/計程車司機/秘書/辦公室人員/銷售人員/飯店櫃臺。英文開口說，音譯寶典。用中文音譯學習英文，不用高學歷也會開口說英語！讓您輕鬆工作上的說英語的需求！

這句日語你用對了嗎

擺脫中文思考的日文學習方式
列舉台灣人學日文最常混淆的各種用法
讓你用「對」的日文順利溝通

雅典文化
書目

永續編號	書名	定價	作者

另類學習系列

S1904	我的菜英文—菲傭溝通篇	180	張瑜凌
S1905	我的菜英文—運將大哥篇	180	張瑜凌
S1906	我的菜英文—旅遊篇	180	張瑜凌
S1907	我的菜英文【單字篇】	180	張瑜凌
S1908	我的菜英文【工作職場篇】(MP3)	250	張瑜凌

生活英語系列

S2301	十句話讓你輕鬆開口說英文	220	張瑜凌
S2302	十句ABC讓你遊遍全球	220	張瑜凌
S2303	十句ABC讓你溝通無障礙	200	張瑜凌
S2304	10句話讓你輕鬆和菲傭溝通(附CD)	250	張瑜凌
S2305	10句話讓你輕鬆當個運將大哥附CD	250	張瑜凌
S2306	10句話讓你當個稱職的女秘書	220	張瑜凌
S2307	10句話讓你輕鬆當個警察大人	250	張瑜凌
S2308	超簡單的旅遊英語(附MP3)	250	張瑜凌
S2309	脫口說英語(MP3)(25開)	299	張瑜凌
S2310	遊學必備1500句(mp3)(25開)	299	張瑜凌

實用會話系列

S2401	十大會話讓你電話溝通沒煩惱	200	張瑜凌
S2402	十大會話讓你求職技巧有一套	200	張瑜凌
S2403	十大會話讓你求職技巧有一套-MP3	250	張瑜凌
S2404	讓你輕鬆接待國外客戶(附CD)	250	張瑜凌

雅典文化

國家圖書館出版品預行編目資料

別再笑,「他媽的」英文怎麼說?/張瑜凌編著.
--初版.--臺北縣汐止市:雅典文化,民100.01
　　面; 公分. -- (全民學英文系列:23)
　　ISBN:978-986-6282-26-3 (平裝)
　1.英語　2.口語　3.句法　4.會話
805.169　　　　　　　　　　　　99022539

全民學英文 **23** 別再笑,「他媽的」英文怎麼說

編 著	張瑜凌
出 版 者	雅典文化事業有限公司
登 記 證	局版北市業字第五七○號
發 行 人	黃玉雲
執 行 編 輯	張瑜凌
編 輯 部	221台北縣汐止市大同路三段194-號9樓
電 子 郵 件	a8823.a1899@msa.hinet.net
電 話	02-86473663
傳 真	02-86473660
郵 撥	18965580雅典文化事業有限公司
法 律 顧 問	中天國際法律事務所 涂成樞、周金成律師
總 經 銷	永續圖書有限公司 221台北縣汐止市大同路三段194-號9樓
電 子 郵 件	yungjiuh@ms45.hinet.net
郵 撥	18669219永續圖書有限公司
網 站	www.foreverbooks.com.tw
電 話	02-86473663
傳 真	02-86473660
ISBN	978-986-6282-26-3
初 版	2011年01月
定 價	NT$ **169**元

雅典文化 讀者回函卡

謝謝您購買這本書。
為加強對讀者的服務，請您詳細填寫本卡，寄回**雅典文化**；
並請務必留下您的E-mail帳號，我們會主動將最近 "好康"
的促銷活動告 訴您，保證值回票價。

書　　名：別再笑，「他媽的」英文怎麼說？
購買書店：＿＿＿＿＿市/縣＿＿＿＿＿＿＿書店
姓　　名：＿＿＿＿＿＿＿　生　日：＿＿＿年＿＿月＿＿日
身分證字號：＿＿＿＿＿＿＿＿＿＿＿＿＿＿＿＿＿＿
電　　話：(私)＿＿＿＿＿(公)＿＿＿＿＿(手機)＿＿＿＿＿
地　　址：□□□＿＿＿＿＿＿＿＿＿＿＿＿＿＿＿＿＿
E - mail：＿＿＿＿＿＿＿＿＿＿＿＿＿＿＿＿＿＿＿
年　　齡：□20歲以下　□21歲~30歲　□31歲~40歲
　　　　　□41歲~50歲　□51歲以上
性　　別：□男 □女　　婚姻：□單身 □已婚
職　　業：□學生　　□大眾傳播　□自由業　□資訊業
　　　　　□金融業　□銷售業　　□服務業　□教職
　　　　　□軍警　　□製造業　　□公職　　□其他
教育程度：□國中以下（含國中）□高中以下（含高中）
　　　　　□大專　　□研究所以上
職 位 別：□在學中　□負責人　□高階主管　□中級主管
　　　　　□一般職員 □專業人員
職 務 別：□學生　□ 管理　　□行銷　　□創意　　□人事、行政
　　　　　□財務、法務　　　□生產　　□工程　　□其他＿＿＿＿
您從何得知本書消息？
　　　　□逛書店　　□報紙廣告　□親友介紹
　　　　□出版書訊　□廣告信函　□廣播節目
　　　　□電視節目　□銷售人員推薦
　　　　□其他＿＿＿＿＿＿＿＿＿＿＿＿＿＿＿＿
您通常以何種方式購書？
　　　　□逛書店　　□劃撥郵購　□電話訂購　□傳真訂購　□信用卡
　　　　□團體訂購　□網路書店　□DM　　　□其他＿＿＿＿＿
看完本書後，您喜歡本書的理由？
　　　　□內容符合期待　□文筆流暢　□具實用性　□插圖生動
　　　　□版面、字體安排適當　　　□內容充實
　　　　□其他＿＿＿＿＿＿＿＿＿＿＿＿＿＿＿＿
看完本書後，您不喜歡本書的理由？
　　　　□內容不符合期待　□文筆欠佳　□內容平平
　　　　□版面、圖片、字體不適合閱讀　□觀念保守
　　　　□其他＿＿＿＿＿＿＿＿＿＿＿＿＿＿＿＿
您的建議：

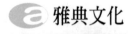